# *Christ[...]*

Yes, it is—

All our stories [...] children at Christmas time, as the adults in their lives try their very best to make the festive season as happy as possible for the little, and not so little, ones concerned, while finding their own special person to love. And sometimes the kids work a little magic of their own, for the best present of all is to become a family.

Our four authors bring you their family traditions from around the world. We visit America with Jessica Matthews, Australia with Meredith Webber, South Africa with Elisabeth Scott and England with Caroline Anderson. The different types of weather in these countries make no difference to the warmth of the Season's Greeting we send to you.

**Dear Reader**

In our household, as in yours, Christmas wouldn't be Christmas without traditions. But whether they remain the same or evolve over the years the practices we cling to make the season special.

During the first years of our marriage, my husband and I would drive thirty miles to a local tree farm to cut our own tree. There's nothing like hearing the crunch of snow beneath your feet, feeling the cold air against your face, and studying each tree for suitability to get even the most bah-humbug person in the mood for the holidays.

That custom gradually gave way to supporting the civic groups who brought freshly cut pines to sell in supermarket parking lots. Sadly enough, after my son was born, his allergies forced us to modify our tradition once again. We compromised by purchasing the most realistic-looking artificial tree that would fit in our living room!

As our children have gotten older, I've gradually turned the task of decorating over to them. Although we once hung shiny bulbs and tinsel, now our ornaments are a mixture of heirloom 'Baby's First Christmas' balls, crocheted snowflakes (courtesy of my sister), paper creations (thanks to school art projects by my son and daughter), sewing figures (gifts from fellow seamstresses), and a hodge-podge of other items made precious by memories.

I'm always amazed at the magic to be found during this special month. We're provided with a window of opportunity to stir hope in our hearts for the times ahead, to seek healing for past hurts in our lives, and to pass our traditions on to the next generation.

My wish for you is to find time in the frantic pace to reflect on and celebrate the reasons for the season. May your dreams all come true. Merry Christmas!

*Jessica Matthews*

# A HEALING SEASON

BY
JESSICA MATTHEWS

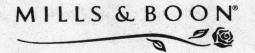

MILLS & BOON®

*MILLS & BOON and MILLS & BOON with the Rose Device
are registered trademarks of the publisher.*

*First published in Great Britain 1997
Harlequin Mills & Boon Limited,
Eton House, 18-24 Paradise Road, Richmond, Surrey TW9 1SR*

© Jessica Matthews 1997

ISBN 0 263 80514 X

*Set in Times 10 on 11 pt. by
Rowland Phototypesetting Limited
Bury St Edmunds, Suffolk*

03-9712-465715-D

*Printed and bound in Great Britain
by Mackays of Chatham PLC, Chatham*

# CHAPTER ONE

*It couldn't be him. It just couldn't.*

Clutching a shoe box filled with lengths of red ribbon and miniature Christmas ornaments to her chest, Libby Brown froze at the sound of the deep voice coming from outside the nurses' lounge. She'd never expected, never *wanted*, to hear the smooth, cultured baritone again.

Surely she was mistaken; surely her memories were faulty, she told herself, willing her heart rate to a normal pace. One of the men who'd been instrumental in changing her life ten years ago couldn't possibly be here at St Nicholas Hospital.

Determined to put her fears to rest, she moved closer to the doorway on silent soft-soled white shoes, straining to hear the conversation. From her place near the corner, she peered into the hallway and caught a glimpse of three people.

The first was Ann Lathrop, the unit manager, who was forty-five and wore a perpetual smile to match her outgoing personality. Eldon Hanover, the administrator whose boyish face contradicted the responsibility on his shoulders, stood next to her in his usual conservative uniform of dark suit, white shirt and multicolored tie.

Her gaze landed on the second man who wore a deep navy suit and who, like Eldon, appeared to be in his mid-thirties. In the space of a heartbeat she studied his profile, noting patrician features, a long, straight nose, firm jawline, high forehead and thick, reddish-brown hair.

Stifling a gasp, she pulled back, anxious to remain hidden. Those few details, including his towering height, matched those she remembered.

And dreamed about in her nightmares.

Libby sagged against the wall. What was Peter Caldwell doing here in Belleville, Nebraska?

The Caldwell she knew had been a graduate student in business administration—a perfect career choice for a man so totally ruthless and unfeeling. Although she paid scant attention to St Nick's gossip mill, she was certain she'd have heard about changes in the management team. Anything with a potential to impact jobs, be it major or minor, generated a flood of speculation about the future.

Maybe he was only visiting, she told herself. Administrators probably toured other facilities to see how they functioned, just as nurses, doctors and other health-care professionals did.

Joni Eller would know the full story, Libby decided. Her best friend and fellow nurse kept her fingers on the pulse of hospital activities as carefully as she did on her patients. She had the most amazing ability to ferret out information before anyone else had an inkling.

The voices grew louder and she straightened. Not in the habit of running from trouble, a small part of her itched for a confrontation, but for her and her son's sake this situation was an exception. If she never met another member of the Caldwell family it would be too soon.

She took a deep breath, mentally plotting her exit as she geared herself for action. Knowing the trio stood in the hallway to her left, she strode from the room on a right-handed course and didn't look back. Her detour would take her on a longer route to reach her patient, but until she knew why Caldwell was here she intended to lie low and blend into the scenery as much as possible.

A blinking light above one door made her hesitate. Officially, she was off duty, but since this shift was shorthanded she hated to make the good-natured Ira Kendrick wait for another staff member to arrive. Knowing how undemanding he was, whatever had prompted him to request assistance must be important.

'What can I do for you?' she asked the eighty-year-old gentlemen who'd had his leg amputated below the knee several days ago. A diabetic, a sore on his foot had become infected to the point where aggressive treatment had been necessary.

'I hate to bother you.' He spoke with traces of a German accent and his lined face wore an apology. 'But I dropped my pen and it rolled under the bed.'

'Let's have a look.' Libby crouched down, spied the pen behind one of the metal legs and retrieved it. 'Here you go.'

'Thank you, my dear.'

She stood. 'Can I get you anything else?'

'Nah, I'm fine,' he said, going back to his crossword puzzle book.

'Did the physical therapist drop in yet?'

He nodded. 'Like I told her, I don't see a reason to go to the trouble and expense of having an artificial leg. Living in the nursing home, I can get by without one.' He winked. 'The lady I keep company with is in a wheelchair, too. Why should I learn to walk when I'll walk alone?'

Libby marveled at his attitude. 'If you have second thoughts. . .'

He patted her hand. 'I won't. Now run along and tend someone who really needs you.'

She grinned. 'See you tomorrow.'

Cautiously she approached the hallway. The corridor was vacant and she breathed a sigh of relief. Several hurried steps and one turn later she arrived at her destination.

'Thought maybe you changed your mind,' Ralph Upton grumbled.

'I got sidetracked.' Too bad Ralph didn't have a portion of Mr Kendrick's good nature.

'Why are you shutting the door?'

'I thought you'd like some privacy,' she prevaricated, leaving the door partially open as a compromise.

Ralph's pale eyes narrowed. 'You're just decorating the tree, right? I mean, you're not going to give me a bath or anything, are you?'

'I'm only here as a visitor.' The word called to mind the man she hoped to avoid and she cringed.

'Whatever.'

Libby placed her box on the bedside table and whipped off the lid. The bright colors and the prospect of preparing for her favorite holiday chased away her latest worries as she began removing ribbon, scissors, wire hooks and a small package of shiny round ornaments. Next, she carried the eighteen-inch potted evergreen from its place in a corner to her temporary workstation.

'Want to help?' she asked.

Ralph shook his gray head and folded his arms, looking like a petulant child. 'This was your idea so you can take care of it. I've done all the Christmas decorating I'm gonna do. Look where it got me.'

'Now, Ralph,' she chided. 'Don't hate the holiday because you broke a few bones getting ready for it. Accidents happen. You could have slipped in your bathtub or fallen on the ice.'

'I could have, but I didn't. If it wasn't for that ridiculous contest the city sponsors every year I wouldn't be in this fix.'

'You mean, if it wasn't for your stubbornness you wouldn't be here,' she corrected. 'Our block committee has a list of volunteers who were more than willing to decorate your house for the Christmas competition. You didn't have to be on your roof, especially with the wind blowing thirty miles an hour.'

'I may be old but I'm not helpless.'

'Of course you're not,' Libby soothed. 'There simply comes a time when it makes good sense to let younger and more agile people handle the physical things.'

'I don't want anyone else on my property. Why, if someone got hurt I'd be sued for every dime I have.'

She let the comment pass as she tied the last red satin bow on a branch. Minutes later the ornaments were hung to her satisfaction, and she stepped back to survey her handiwork.

'What do you think of my creation?'

Ralph turned his head in her direction, the scowl on his sixty-five-year-old weatherbeaten face obvious. It's OK.'

Determined to coax more of a response, she studied the tree again. 'Maybe it could use a few more bows. I've got some red and white polka-dotted ribbon at home—'

'Good gosh, girl. Polka dots?' He sounded aghast. 'It looks fine like it is.'

As compliments went, it wasn't the greatest but, having been Ralph's next-door neighbor since she and her son Kyle had moved to town seven years ago, it was high praise. He'd always been gruff, but she'd soon learned that his surly manner was a ploy to keep people at a distance. Since then she'd made it her goal to include him in as many activities as possible.

Although he fussed and fumed, the occasional look of pride on his face as he assumed the role of surrogate grandparent to her young son told her that he enjoyed both the attention and honor. Provided, of course, she didn't overdo it.

Libby tapped her chin. 'If you're sure. . .'

'I'm positive,' he said with vehemence. 'Course, I don't understand why you had to decorate my tree for Christmas when it's only the fifteenth of November. Gosh, girlie, most folks haven't put away their Halloween stuff yet. And don't forget Thanksgiving Day is coming up at the end of the month.'

'You're right. I *have* forgotten about the pilgrims and Indians celebrating their first year in the New World. I'll take these bows off and replace them with paper turkeys in honor of the holiday.'

Ralph sputtered. 'Turkeys? You're going to make a *turkey* tree? Forget it!' He shook his head. 'If you do I ain't takin' it home. Good gosh, a turkey tree. What'll you think of next?'

She grinned. 'Well, there's Valentine's Day in February, St Patrick's Day in March and, of course, Easter. That means hearts, shamrocks, bunnies and eggs.'

'I'll keep the bows, thank you.' He narrowed his eyes. 'You really weren't going to tie poultry on it, were you?'

Her smile grew broader. 'What do you think?'

'I think you've been spending way too much time with that busybody, Sylvia,' he grumbled. 'The neighborhood hasn't been the same since she moved in five years ago come January.'

'Just think how boring it would be if she lived someplace else,' Libby commented, tidying the room.

'I'd call it peaceful.'

She turned away to place the plant in a prominent corner and hide her grin. Living between the two people who thrived on the sparks they struck off each other was sometimes difficult but never dull. In fact, she suspected it was more a game than true animosity.

'My decorations are just the thing this tree needed. Doesn't your room seem brighter now?'

'*Smells* is more like it,' Ralph grumbled.

Undaunted by his familiar pessimism, she grinned. 'You must have broken your nose at the same time you broke your leg. Anyone who can't tell the difference between a fresh pine scent and hospital disinfectant has to have something wrong.'

'Still don't know why you bothered. The thing will shrivel up and die before I'm outa this place.'

'Nonsense.' She gathered up the remnants of her supplies and tossed them into a small box. 'You're leaving tomorrow and I'm willing to guarantee the tree is hardy enough to last the next twenty-four hours.'

He replied with a grunt.

'You could have gone home sooner, you know, if you'd let me call your son—'

'No! We parted ways ten years ago. If he wants to know how I'm doin' he knows where to find me.'

According to Sylvia, the rift in the Upton family centered around the refusal of Ralph's son to continue in the family tradition of bricklaying. Yet, Libby knew Ralph felt the loss because she'd seen the torment in his eyes at various times when Kyle was in the old man's presence. Sensing Ralph's growing agitation, she approached the bed.

'Any pain? Everything OK?' she asked, checking the fingers and toes peeking out from the casts while mentally reviewing his clinical picture—a clean break of the radius in his arm and a more complicated comminuted or multiple-piece fracture of the femur. While the orthopedist had set Ralph's arm in surgery, using a closed reduction technique, his leg required open reduction—opening the skin so the physician could visually align the fragments of bone together.

'Peachy,' he said, his sarcasm obvious as he stared at the ceiling.

An unexpected voice came from the doorway. 'I see your attitude hasn't improved since I left yesterday.'

Libby turned and greeted Ralph's visitor, sixty-year-old Sylvia Posy. Ralph groaned.

Apparently undaunted by his lack of enthusiasm, Sylvia bustled in on a cloud of lavender and sank onto the vinyl-cushioned chair next to his bed. She placed a small tin in his lap. 'I figured you were giving the nurses problems so I brought your favorite cookies to sweeten you up—oatmeal butterscotch.'

Ralph pressed the button to raise the head of his bed. 'Well, now. Why didn't you say so?'

Libby exchanged a wink with Sylvia. 'I'll leave you two alone to visit.'

'Working late, hon?' Sylvia asked.

'I went off duty thirty minutes ago. I stayed to decorate Ralph's tree.'

'It looks very festive,' Sylvia declared.

Libby tucked the box in the crook of one arm. 'I'd better go. I promised Kyle we'd work on our own decorations before dark. I also want to talk to the couple who've moved into the old Appleton house about participating in the city competition.'

'It isn't a couple,' Ralph interjected. 'A man and his daughter moved in. He doesn't seem too friendly, either.'

Sylvia shot him an exasperated look. 'And how would you be the judge of that, Mr Grump?'

''Cos I've seen him, Mrs Nosy. Must have some fancy job 'cos just as I started to say hello his cell phone bleeped. He went inside without so much as an "excuse me". Whoever he is won't be as easy to convince as I was.'

Considering how it had taken weeks of relentless badgering before Ralph would agree to get in the spirit of the contest, Libby doubted it. 'Then I'll have to be my most persuasive. In the meantime, behave yourselves. Ralph, I'll see you tomorrow.'

She hurried to the staff lounge, slipped a knee-length woolen coat over her white uniform jumpsuit, slung her purse over one shoulder, grabbed her lunchbag and the near-empty shoebox, then ambled toward the stairs.

Passing the bank of patient elevators, she saw Joni standing alone, wearing her down-filled parka and jabbing the button.

Libby stopped. 'Working late?'

Joni's face lit up. 'Had some paperwork to finish. You know how Rita is.'

Hired as a floating nurse, Libby had worked with nearly every RN and on most of the units including the paeds wing where Joni was now assigned. Rita's propensity for perfection was legendary; Libby dreaded stints on her ward for that reason. Although she knew she did a good job and was confident in her abilities, having someone watch over her shoulder and pounce on every undotted 'i' wasn't Libby's idea of pleasant working conditions.

'What about you?' Joni asked.

'I stayed to visit my neighbor who broke several bones the other day. By the way, are we getting a new person in administration? I saw Eldon Hanover showing some guy around our unit earlier.' She hoped she sounded more nonchalant than she felt.

Joni shook her head. 'Not to my knowledge. It was probably the new family practice doctor who's going to work with Drs Moore and Downey.'

Libby relaxed. The man she knew didn't have enough compassion to become a doctor.

'I think his name is Caldwell. Peter Caldwell.'

Libby tensed. Lots of people have the same name, she told herself in an effort to quiet her inner alarm. It was a mere coincidence the two men resembled each other.

'I understand he's an old college buddy of Hanover's,' Joni continued. 'Dr Caldwell got his MBA before he studied medicine. In fact, he finished his residency this past summer.'

A lump of absolute dismay clogged Libby's throat. It *was* him—the same Peter Caldwell who'd condoned his cousin's irresponsibility. How could life be so cruel? Hadn't she and her family already paid their dues? As far as she was concerned, this continent wasn't large enough for both of them, much less this community of thirty thousand people.

Her stomach churned.

'He's taking Dr Greenburg's place in Dr Moore and Downey's family practice group,' Joni added. 'I hope he'll be easier to work with than old Greenburg was. Anyway, ride down with me and I'll fill you in on the rest of the gossip.'

The grin Libby summoned was half-hearted. 'You can talk while we're taking the stairs.'

Joni groaned. 'That's four flights! Have pity on my poor feet, will you? Surely you can stand a thirty-second trip.'

Suffering from mild claustrophobia, Libby avoided tight spaces whenever possible, although she could cope well enough if she had no other choice. She preferred the stairs because there were windows on each level, but her friend's hangdog expression made her give in.

'I suppose I can. Just this once.'

While they waited Joni counted off on her fingers. 'Dr Downey is taking a leave of absence, starting next week; he's going on a cruise. Next, Mona in Obstetrics is pregnant and Jill's husband served divorce papers on her today.'

Libby grimaced. 'How rotten.' Although she'd had moments of regret over her single status, news like this made her count her blessings.

'But the most interesting and the most scary news is. . .' Joni moved closer to whisper in Libby's ear, 'The business people are talking layoffs.'

'Oh, yeah?' Libby studied the overhead panel and saw the elevators hadn't moved. She jabbed the 'down' arrow again.

'You don't seem very upset.'

Seeing Peter Caldwell after all these years and knowing she had to share not only a town but also her place of employment made everything else pale in comparison. 'Should I be?'

Joni rolled her eyes and shook her head, her action having no effect on her exceedingly short white-blonde tresses. Although Libby envied the girl's easy-care hairdo, she preferred her own shoulder-length style and the versatility her latest home perm had given her.

'You know what always happens. The last hired are the first to go and you, my dear, unfortunately fall in that category.'

'There were dire predictions a year ago about a hiring freeze and they recruited me as soon as I graduated from training. Someone's always preaching gloom and doom.'

'This time, it isn't a prediction. It's fairly certain.'

' "Fairly certain" and "certain" aren't the same thing,' Libby reminded her.

'This came straight out of Hanover's office. It's accurate.'

Libby grinned at her friend's insistence. 'How do you hear everything before it happens?'

Joni tossed her head, the row of diamond studs along the outer edge of her ear glittering under the harsh hospital lighting, and winked. 'Are you sure you want to know?'

'You're right. I'd rather not,' Libby replied wryly. 'Besides, if the board of directors has decided to delete staff positions, worrying won't change a thing. Tomorrow will take care of itself.' Having juggled motherhood, an education and a job since she was eighteen, she'd learned not to look for trouble. It usually came on its own.

The problem facing her was a prime example. Peter Caldwell had to be avoided at all costs.

It might not be too difficult, she decided. On those occasions when she or Kyle visited their family doctor they rarely encountered a physician other than Dr Downey. Their chances of running into Peter even if he was part of the same group practice were slim.

As for the hospital, she'd have to engage in some creative thinking. While she wouldn't be able to evade him totally if she cared for one of his patients, she'd do her best to keep their contact to a minimum.

In all, with a little sleuthing, careful planning and a fair amount of luck, their paths would rarely cross. She'd simply be another of the nameless, faceless mass of hospital employees.

Her confidence restored, Libby studied the row of numbers above the elevator. 'If our ride doesn't show up soon I'm taking the stairs. I told Kyle I'd be home by four o'clock and it's nearly four now.' Just as she finished speaking one elevator began its descent.

In a few seconds a distinct 'ding' announced its arrival. 'Finally,' Libby said, stepping back to allow the passengers room to exit.

The door slid open and the sight of two men made her feel as if she'd stepped into the lion's den. One she ignored, the other made her heart pound.

Peter Caldwell.

The smile on her face froze and her breath caught in her throat. She prayed for him to step off the elevator. To her dismay, neither man made a move.

Joni nudged her forward and she advanced on leaden feet, stealing surreptitious glances at Peter.

Other than a few threads of gray and crow's-feet around his eyes, he hadn't aged significantly over the past ten years.

And yet this man didn't seem to be the same Peter Caldwell. He still appeared self-assured, but without the cockiness and hard-heartedness she remembered. His eyes held a quality she couldn't quite identify, something akin to sadness. Had life thrown him a few curves—a few problems that the Caldwell name and fortune couldn't solve?

His obsidian eyes bored into hers, but she didn't see a flicker of recognition. Thankful for that, she turned her back toward him. No sense in allowing him the opportunity to refresh his memory. Even so, she'd changed drastically since their dramatic encounter— her hair was now long and curly, contacts had replaced her glasses and her skin was tanned from being outdoors with an active boy. She'd dropped twenty-five pounds as her activity level rose until finally she had the right curves for her twenty-seven year-old five-foot-six-inch frame.

Her hair color, however, remained the same. It was still the shade of a fawn's coat and, because she liked it, she'd refused to alter it.

For a few seconds she wished she had.

She took a deep breath, fear heightening her sense of smell. The scent of sandalwood and soap filled her nostrils—a fragrance so distinctive it could only belong to one man.

Eldon spoke, interrupting her racing thoughts. 'By the way, I saw Tom Bozeman a few weeks ago. You remember him. He was in our "Principles of Management" class at KU.'

'Short, stocky guy?' Peter asked.

'That's right.'

Although she'd believed Joni's information, hearing the two men discuss their association with the University of Kansas—the same campus she'd attended for two semesters—hammered home the unforeseen turn of events.

Certain that reminiscing about their college days would trigger Caldwell's memory, she waited with bated breath for him to address her.

Tense with anticipation, nausea overtook her and she clamped her teeth together. With shaky fingers she rubbed the back of her neck, feeling the sweat trickle between her shoulder blades.

Would this ride never end?

Joni moved closer, a wrinkle of worry between her eyebrows. 'You OK?' she whispered.

Libby nodded.

'Is something wrong, ladies?' Peter asked in his resonant voice.

There certainly is, Libby thought, praying for escape while staring at the floor numbers near the ceiling. Through sheer force of will she shook her head, and sent Joni a silent request to corroborate her answer.

Joni turned and smiled at him. 'Not at all.'

What seemed like hours later, but was a minute at the most, the elevator settled on the ground level. Before the doors had fully opened Libby bolted through and rushed to the exit closest to the employee parking lot. Outside the building she closed her eyes and lifted her face to the late afternoon sun, savoring the crisp air against her overheated skin.

The hand on her shoulder was light and comforting.

'I'll be fine in a minute, Joni,' she said without moving a muscle.

'I'm glad to hear it,' a familiar masculine voice answered. 'In the meantime, just take deep breaths.'

Her eyelids shot open. Peter's face hovered a few inches above hers. She braced herself for the worst— recognition—but none came. The only thing glimmering in his dark eyes was compassion. . .and undisguised interest.

Joni came into her line of vision. 'Gosh, Lib. I didn't realize you hated riding the elevator so much or I'd never have asked you.'

'Get her some water, please,' he ordered.

'Wait!' Libby called, hating to be left alone with him, but she was too late. Her friend had disappeared.

'Claustrophobia?' he asked.

Libby nodded. In actuality, she'd been too overwhelmed by his presence to notice the close confines, but she wasn't about to admit that sordid detail. She allowed the excuse to stand unchallenged.

Joni returned, carrying a paper cup. Libby sipped the cold water, unable to avoid Peter's mesmerizing gaze. He was as handsome, as virile, as she remembered.

'Your color's coming back,' he said. 'I don't think you'll need me.'

Libby gulped the rest of her drink, berating herself for falling under his spell for even a few seconds. She'd never need him, not as long as she—or Kyle—lived.

'Thanks, Doctor,' Joni answered.

The awe in Joni's voice made Libby want to poke her friend in the ribs. Caldwell men possessed an unusual ability to induce women's adoration—the society pages proved it. Her sister had succumbed to the Caldwell charm and paid the price.

So had Libby.

'Then I'll leave you. Ladies, it's been a pleasure.' With that, he strode back into the building.

'Wow!'

Joni's dreamy expression rekindled Libby's anger and she turned on her. 'How could you ask him to follow me?' she ground out.

Joni blinked. 'I didn't. He rushed past me like he was on his way to a Code Blue.'

Libby groaned. This was worse than she'd thought. So much for her plan to keep a low profile.

'Honestly, Lib. Why are you so upset? Just think, you've made a memorable impression on the newest bachelor in town. Every single woman in this hospital will be envious when they hear what happened.'

Libby narrowed her eyes. 'Who said he's not married?'

'He wasn't wearing a ring. Didn't you notice?'

Libby squared her shoulders and straightened to her full height. 'This episode had better not be mentioned. Not now, not ever, not to anyone. Do I make myself clear?'

Joni appeared affronted. 'Geez. Don't get your stethoscope in a knot. I won't breathe a syllable of this to a soul.'

'Promise?'

Joni raised one hand. 'I promise.' She lowered her arm and grinned. 'Mark my words. Dr Caldwell won't forget you.'

Joni's predictions echoed Libby's fears and she cringed at the frightful prospect.

# CHAPTER TWO

'HEY, Mom? Can Sam help us?'

Perched on a stepladder, Libby uncoiled a strand of Christmas lights along the edge of the shingled roof. Maneuvering carefully to maintain her balance, she clipped the coated wires to the steel rain guttering. She couldn't afford to end up in the hospital like Ralph but, being on the block's decorating committee, she wanted to finish her own home before she tackled anyone else's project. Besides, the weather was too nice to spend the evening indoors.

'If it's OK with—' The screen door interrupted her sentence as he scampered inside.

'His mother,' she finished. Although she and Kyle had established a routine over the years and didn't need the extra pair of hands, she was anxious to meet Kyle's new friend. Some might call her too strict, but she screened Kyle's playmates for his safety and her own peace of mind. Still, she'd been lucky. Her son's standards for buddies, at least so far, had been as high as her own.

She climbed down, breathing in the crisp autumn air. Although the temperature had dropped slightly since she'd come home an hour earlier, the long-sleeved red plaid shirt and black knit top underneath kept her warm enough.

The door banged again, heralding Kyle's return. 'No answer. I'll try again later.' He stood next to her and stared at the roof. 'I think we should leave our lights up year round.'

'But preparing is half the fun of the holiday.' She moved the ladder a few more feet. 'Do you want a Santa Claus in your yard in July?'

'I guess not.'

She slung one arm around his shoulders and gave him a gentle squeeze. At the rate he was growing he'd reach her own height in a few years.

'Besides, we make such a great team we'll be finished in no time.' She rumpled his hair. Although she preferred to believe the reddish highlights came from a distant ancestor in her genetic pool, after seeing Peter she knew better. Those rich hues were courtesy of his father.

'Why don't you set the candy canes around the porch?'

'OK.' He ran into the garage. The screech of unoiled wheels interrupted the evening quiet minutes before he appeared, pulling his well-used Red Flyer wagon. One tire wobbled in time to the squeaks and she sighed. Climbing the ladder, she mentally added another project to her list.

The noise stopped. While Libby tended her own tasks she monitored Kyle's progress. He inserted the curved plastic canes into the ground, not only spacing them at precise intervals with the help of his metal tape measure but also measuring to place each one at an identical height. She grinned. Although she was conscientious he hadn't learned that degree of meticulousness from her.

For the first time she wondered if Kyle had inherited his propensity for building from his father. Impossible, she decided. Bryce Caldwell wasn't the sort of man who dirtied his hands with anything. Kyle's interest in tools was simply common to inquisitive boys.

Now that she'd thought about the other half of Kyle's family tree, Peter Caldwell's face danced across her vision. Peter's and Bryce's fathers were twins and their sons' physical likeness was uncanny.

Luckily, she, too, had high cheek-bones and dark eyes, which caused many people to remark about their mother-son resemblance. The rest of Kyle's features were a blend of both Brown and Caldwell attributes, creating a boy who had the potential to be a heartthrob like the other Caldwell men.

One thing was certain, however. She would make sure he had more character than his father. Whatever mistakes Kyle made Kyle would assume responsibility. He wouldn't send a relative to straighten out his problems like Bryce Caldwell had sent Peter.

Still, now wasn't the time for soul-searching or a trip down memory lane. She had lights to deal with and it would be dark soon.

Springing into action, she moved the ladder and climbed the rungs again. Up and down she went until her leg muscles burned from exertion. By the time she'd finished and had both feet firmly planted on the ground her skin glistened with a fine sheen of perspiration.

'I'm gonna call Sam one more time,' Kyle said.

'Flip the switch on your way,' she told him. 'Let's see if everything works.'

He complied and the lights twinkled merrily. As she studied the row of blinking colors a young voice came from behind. 'I don't see the green ones.'

Libby swung around and saw a seven-or eight-year-old girl standing on the sidewalk, wearing blue jeans, a denim jacket and Colorado Rockies baseball cap. Dirt smudged her face and grass stains covered her knees.

'Hi, there,' Libby said.

'Hi. The green ones aren't working,' the youngster repeated.

Libby glanced at her roof. 'You're right. They're

not.' Inwardly, she groaned. Every bulb had flashed perfectly when she'd tested them before she began. The height didn't bother her, but the muscles in her calves were protesting their mistreatment. Now she had to crawl back on the ladder and find the culprit by a painstaking process of elimination, which in times past had taken what had seemed like for ever.

The door slammed. 'Sam still doesn't answer, Mom.' Kyle bounded into the yard with the exuberance of youth. He stopped short, a huge grin on his face. 'Hey, you're here! No wonder I couldn't get you on the phone.'

Libby turned and saw only the little girl. '*You're* Sam?'

Sam stuffed her fists into her pockets, dug the toe of one dirty sneaker in the dead grass and nodded. 'My real name's Samantha. But I don't let anyone call me that. It sounds sissy.'

Once Libby recovered from her initial shock at Sam's gender she understood why Kyle had chosen her for a playmate. As long as Sam shared his interests of outdoor sports, bug collecting, fishing and anything that involved getting dirty, she would be an acceptable comrade. From the looks of her, she embraced Kyle's nine-year-old passions.

Libby tried to be diplomatic. 'Well, I think Samantha is a beautiful name. Elegant, in fact.' Sam's dark brown eyes flashed with apparent indignation and her rosebud mouth turned into a hard line. Libby continued, 'But I'll remember to call you Sam.'

'Wanna help me string the lights along the candy canes?' Kyle asked his new friend.

'OK.' With Sam's good humor apparently restored, the two children moved off to work together while Libby returned to her own task. Keeping a watchful eye on her helpers, she listened to Kyle with amusement.

'First, we have to plug them in and see if they're working,' he instructed his assistant, kneeling on the ground next to the red-and-white-striped stakes. 'Then we slide the wires in the notches, like so.'

The streetlamp clicked on in the dusk. 'It's getting dark, guys,' Libby called. 'Find a stopping point. Tomorrow's another day.'

'OK,' they chorused.

By the time Libby had found and replaced the defective green bulb the children had finished stringing their lights along the porch. The trio stood back to appraise their efforts.

'It's beautiful,' Sam breathed, wearing a look of rapture on her face. 'The most beautiful thing I've ever seen.'

'Don't you put up decorations at Christmas?' Kyle asked, his voice filled with amazement.

Sam shook her head. 'My daddy doesn't have time. We have a tree, though.'

'You should see ours,' Kyle bragged. 'We go to the Christmas tree farm and cut down our own. It goes almost to the ceiling.'

Sam's eyes grew round. 'Really? Ours comes out of a box in the basement.'

'It's *fake*?' Kyle wrinkled his nose.

'Artificial trees are nice,' Libby inserted diplomatically.

Sam nodded. 'Daddy says it's just my size, too.'

'That small?' Kyle said, disgust wrinkling his features. 'Are you poor or something?'

'Oh, no. Daddy has lots of money. He says trees in the house cause fires and make a big mess for Grandma Bridges.'

'Do they, Mom? Make a mess?' Kyle asked.

'They can,' she answered, remembering her own battles with fallen pine needles. 'That's one of the reasons why it's important to water the tree.'

Sam turned to Kyle. 'Do you have Christmas cookies and go caroling and see Santa Claus?'

'Sure. Don't you?'

Sam shook her head. 'We don't hang lights from our house neither.'

Sam's father ranked in the same class as Ebenezer Scrooge, Libby decided. Surpassed him, in fact. 'You must do something special for the holiday,' she coaxed.

Sam screwed up her face in thought until she shook her head again. 'I spend Christmas Eve at my grandma and grandpa's. Santa fills my stocking there when he brings my presents.'

'Your mom doesn't do *nothing*?' Kyle sounded incredulous.

Surprised by Sam's revelation, Libby allowed Kyle's grammar slip to go by uncorrected.

Sam shook her head. 'The angels took her to heaven when I was little. Daddy said it happened close to Christmas.'

No wonder the man avoided reminders of the season. Instantly Libby softened her opinion of Sam's father and made a decision. Christmas was for children— children of all ages—and she refused to allow this child to be deprived any longer.

'If you'd like, I can always use another kitchen helper when it's time to make our special treats.'

Sam's dark eyes shone. She bobbed her head and jumped for joy, dislodging her cap. It fell, revealing boyishly cut light brown hair.

'Of course, your dad has to agree,' Libby added.

'He will,' Sam said confidently, replacing her cap.

'Then it's settled.' Another streetlamp clicked on and

Libby glanced at the luminous dial of her discount-store watch. 'It's almost dark. Where do you live, Sam? Maybe I should drive you home.'

Sam pointed to the west. 'My house is just over there. The big one on the corner.'

Libby glanced in the direction Sam indicated. 'So you're the new family on the block. I'd planned to drop in this evening and talk to your par—your father, about the city's Christmas lighting contest. If you'll be home, that is.'

Sam's head bobbed up and down. 'We will. O' course he'll prob'ly say no about the Christmas stuff, but I sure hope you can convince him. I'd like our house to be as pretty as yours.'

Libby smiled at Sam's serious expression. 'I'll do my best,' she said, remembering Ralph's comment about the man being unfriendly. Yet if she could convince Ralph to participate she could convince Sam's father.

Several minutes later, after watching Sam enter the yard of the Victorian-style home four houses down, Libby and Kyle gathered their equipment and stashed the boxes inside the garage.

'Come, Kyle. Supper, spelling words, then bedtime.'

'Aw, Mom. I know 'em good enough.'

'Then it won't take long to write them, will it?'

His face was a picture of misery. 'I guess not.'

After a meal of chili simmered all day in the crockpot and home-made cinnamon rolls Libby washed the bowls while Kyle wrote his list of words.

Once he finished he showed her his paper. 'Can I go with you?'

Libby smiled at her son's enthusiasm. She studied his correctly spelled list, then picked up a home-made cherry pie as a welcome-to-the-neighborhood gift.

'Grab a jacket. It's cool.' She snapped her fingers together. 'I should have asked Sam what her dad's name is. Did she tell you?'

'Yeah, but I don't 'member.'

'What does he do for a living?'

'I didn't ask.'

Oh, well. She'd find out soon enough. They set out at a brisk walk, Kyle slipping his small hand into hers. No matter what personal feelings she possessed regarding the Caldwells, this was one Caldwell she'd loved with all her heart from the moment she laid eyes on him. She'd never regretted her decision to help her sister raise Kyle, or to take over the task by herself.

The Victorian house loomed ahead, with light streaming from several windows on each floor. She stopped near the picket fence to gaze at the building. In her mind's eye, she pictured every overhang, every piece of gingerbread trim and every turret sparkling with strings of twinkling bulbs.

What fun to decorate, she thought, envious of the owner. Some day *she* wanted a home like this one— filled with history, memories and character. A place like this needed people—lots of them. How unfortunate the structure's potential was wasted on a man who, even though she sympathized with his pain, shunned the season's joys.

'Pretty neat place. Huh, Mom?'

She gazed upon her son and tweaked his right ear. 'Yeah, but not nearly as cozy as ours.'

A minute later they stood on the wooden porch and Kyle stepped forward to press the doorbell. Chimes signaled their presence and soon the sound of running feet and a childish 'I'll get it' came forth.

Sam flung open the door. Her feet were bare and she still wore the disreputable jeans, but her happy face was scrubbed clean and her hair neatly combed. 'Hi, Mrs Brown,' she said, motioning them inside. 'I told my dad you were coming. He'll be right here.' She eyed the pie plate in Libby's hand. 'Is that for us?'

Libby smiled and handed it to the girl. 'You bet.'

'We love cherry pie,' Sam said, carrying the dish away as if it were the crown jewels.

Libby and Kyle glanced around the foyer, which was almost the size of their home's living room. An L-shaped staircase directly ahead led to the second floor, its oak bannister polished to a glossy shine. A coat rack stood in one corner, and next to it a wooden bench. The seat obviously lifted to hold winter-wear since the fringe from a hot pink neck scarf hung over the edge.

She envisioned a beautiful seven-foot Scotch pine in another corner, covered with burgundy and gold ornaments, bows and beads and Victorian Santas. With a snowy white satin-gowned angel perched on top.

The click of heavy footsteps—a man's tread—grew louder on the hardwood floor. Libby squared her shoulders, drew a deep breath and settled her mouth into a wide smile. She owed it to Sam to be her most convincing.

Several seconds passed before her nose catalogued the sandalwood scent in the air as familiar, and she felt the first stirrings of panic. It burst into full bloom as she recognized the man who followed Samantha and had a white flour-sacking dishtowel slung over one massive shoulder. Her smile wavered.

This wasn't the faceless Mr Bridges she'd expected. This was Peter Caldwell.

'Daddy, this is Mrs Brown. You remember Kyle.'

He addressed the boy. 'How are you, young man?'

'Fine.'

Humor lit Peter's eyes as his gaze landed on Libby. 'A pleasure to meet you, Mrs Brown. Officially, that is.'

Panic closed Libby's throat. She wasn't about to tell him she'd never been married.

'Her name is Libby,' Kyle said helpfully. 'It's a nickname—'

She finished his statement before he said more than she wanted revealed, 'Everyone uses. I didn't realize you were Sam's—Samantha's—father. She mentioned her grandmother's name was Bridges and I assumed—'

'Mrs Bridges is our housekeeper,' Peter said, a twinkle in his eyes. '"Grandma" is purely an honorary title.'

'I see. Well, Kyle didn't tell me that he'd met you.'

'You didn't ask, Mom,' her son defended himself.

As Kyle stood next to Peter Libby saw what she thought was blatantly obvious. The hues of Kyle's hair matched the color of Samantha's and Peter's far better than it did her own. Her wishes went winging to heaven.

*Don't let anyone notice.*

'My daughter has talked about you constantly since she came home.'

All coherent thought fled. Escape became her sole objective. 'Yes, well, she's a sweet girl,' she answered, wincing at her lame remark. 'Anyway, welcome to the neighborhood. Kyle? Let's go.'

She used a firm tone that meant business. This time, however, Kyle didn't co-operate.

'But, Mom! Weren't you going to ask about the contest?' His dark eyes were wide with surprise—eyes that bore more of a resemblance to Peter Caldwell and his daughter than she wanted to admit.

'We've caught them at a bad moment. I'll talk to Dr Caldwell later.' She stepped toward the door, tugging her son with her.

'You aren't interrupting,' Peter said. 'The dishes are clean and waiting to be put away.'

Libby was ready to decline, but the droop in Sam's shoulders and the disappointment in the little girl's eyes forced her to reconsider. Hoping she wouldn't regret her hasty decision, she turned to face Peter. 'If you're sure,' she said.

She stiffened, waiting once again for recognition to spark in his eyes. Luckily, once again she was relieved to find only friendliness in his gaze.

'Positive. Have a seat.' He motioned as he stepped closer to the doorway.

Wondering at her apparent loss of common sense and self-preservation, Libby allowed Sam to take her hand and tug her forward.

The room she found herself in was warm and inviting. The hunter-green sofa and recliners matched the co-ordinating hues in the paisley-print wallpaper.

A corner of the evening newspaper peeked out from under several typewritten pages scattered across the polished oak coffee-table. The television remote lay next to his open suitcase-style briefcase. Obviously, the television itself was hidden in the cabinet along on the north wall.

A brass screen shaped like a fan covered the fireplace opening. Judging from Kyle's widened eyes, he, too, was impressed. How perfect for Christmas stockings and greenery, unlike their own cardboard fireplace with its painted bricks and fire which she dug out of storage in honor of the Christmas season.

She forced her attention to the issue at hand. 'Have you heard about our city-wide block competition?'

'Only in passing,' he said, sinking into the over-stuffed chair opposite her place on the sofa.

'The people on participating streets decorate their

property for the season. Each section is judged for originality, aesthetic quality and so forth.

'First, second and third place ribbons are given to every homeowner and/or tenant as his or her prize. In case you haven't noticed, Christmas is Belleville's favorite holiday. Our Elf's Workshop just south of town opens the day after Thanksgiving and a lot of tourists drive through on their way to visit.'

'I see.'

'Daddy? Can we put lights on our house like everyone else?'

Peter stared at his daughter, his well-formed mouth twisted in apology. 'I don't know, sweetie. It sounds like something nice but I don't have the time.'

Libby wanted to rise, thank him for listening and rush through the doorway before another minute passed, but she forced herself to remain. This was for Sam, she told herself. She couldn't let the little girl down.

'We have a group of volunteers who are willing to string a few lights for the people who would like to take part but can't. If you're interested we could add your name to the list.'

He frowned.

'We wouldn't do anything without prior approval,' she hastened to explain. 'Although everyone purchases their own decorations, if you don't own any I can loan you a plywood Mr and Mrs Santa Claus to stand beside your porch. I'm sure we can borrow a few more things from the neighbors, too.'

'Please, Daddy? *Please?*' Sam begged.

A slow grin crossed Peter's face—a grin which made him seem more human than the arrogant and unapproachable man she remembered from so long ago. 'I suppose.'

Sam clapped her hands and jumped on his lap to give

him a hug and a kiss. 'Goody. Thank you, thank you.'

He enfolded her in his embrace. 'You're welcome, Sammie.'

The love he had for his daughter was obvious and a lump formed in Libby's throat. She looked away to glance at Kyle. The envy on his face was unmistakable and her chest tightened with emotion.

She swallowed hard. 'People usually have their houses ready in time for the lighting ceremony at the courthouse square on the day after Thanksgiving. If you need or want help talk to Leroy Weiser. He's our section chairman and lives across the street.'

Peter nestled Samantha under his arm. 'OK.'

Libby rose. 'Since that's settled and it's getting close to bedtime, we'll be on our way.'

'Ours, too,' he said. 'Sounds like you have the same sleeping habits as we do. Early to bed and early to rise.'

Her face warmed. Discussing beds with the most handsome man she'd encountered in a long time wasn't wise. He was, after all, a Caldwell. 'I suppose so.'

He followed them to the door. 'Thanks for coming. And for the pie, Libby.'

The gleam in his eyes, coupled with the sound of her name in his deep voice, was totally unnerving. She was woman enough to find his interest flattering, but this particular man's was worrisome.

'You're welcome,' she said in a cool but polite tone of dismissal.

Kyle tugged on her arm. 'Mom,' he whispered. 'Let's go.'

The note of fear in his voice caught her attention and she glanced at him. He stared back, his bloodstained fingers pinching his nostrils together.

Libby dug in her pocket for a tissue, but came up empty.

Obviously aware of Kyle's distress, Peter thrust a white handkerchief into his hand. 'Take mine.'

Kyle tipped his head forward, holding the large piece of linen to his nose as he clamped it closed.

'Here,' Peter said, guiding Kyle a few steps to the wooden bench. 'Breathe through your mouth.'

Kyle nodded. He glanced at Libby, his eyes begging for comfort. She moved closer to place her hand on his back.

Peter studied the boy. 'This happens often?'

'Not really. It just seems so,' she said, sitting on the seat next to him. 'Dr Downey says not to worry. He thinks it has to do with the humidity levels and dry mucous membranes.'

'Is he prone to sinus infections?'

'No more so than any other child. Kyle's gone through a whole series of tests and our doctor hasn't found anything significant.'

Libby checked her watch. 'That's five minutes. Shall we see how you're doing?'

Kyle nodded and slowly released his hold. No signs of blood appeared and she smiled. 'It's stopped,' she said.

He started to return the handkerchief, but Peter forestalled him. 'Keep it for now,' he advised. 'You might need it on the way home.'

Pressing the wadded fabric to his nose, Kyle said, 'Thanks.'

Libby ushered her son to the door. 'We'd better go. Good night, Sam. Dr Caldwell.'

While they hurried home Libby prided herself on her success—their block now had one hundred per cent participation and Peter had no inkling about Kyle's identity. She planned to keep it that way.

After a quick bath, a bedtime story and night-time

prayers Libby brought up the subject which was preying on her mind.

'When did you meet Sam's father?'

'A few days ago at school. He offered me a ride home, but I told him that I wasn't allowed to go with strangers.'

'I'm glad you remembered our rule.'

'Dr Caldwell said he understood and hoped we wouldn't be strangers for long. He's pretty neat, don't you think?'

'I suppose so.' If she'd met Peter Caldwell for the first time today she'd agree unequivocally. The concern he'd given her at the hospital and his love for his daughter were enough to bowl over any woman. Unfortunately, her opinion of him had been formed years ago and was set in stone.

'Sam is lucky to have a dad.'

She tucked the covers around her son's flannel-clad shoulders and sat next to him on the bed. 'Yes, she is. But she probably thinks you're lucky to have a mother.'

Kyle nodded, his face solemn.

'I'd like for you to have a father, too, but it hasn't worked out.'

'I'll be ten next summer. Do you think you can find a dad for me before I grow up?'

'These things can't be rushed,' she said, more aware of the time passing than he realized. 'Who knows when the right one will come along? In the meantime, the two of us are doing OK, aren't we?'

'Yeah. Except Sam has grandparents, too, and I don't.'

'You have Ralph and Sylvia. Hasn't Ralph taken you fishing, and doesn't Sylvia bake cookies for you?'

He appeared to consider the matter. 'I guess those are things a grandpa and grandma would do,' he said, before rolling onto his side. 'G'night.'

She kissed his forehead before rising. 'Sleep well.' At the doorway she clicked off the light and left the door ajar.

After rinsing out Peter's handkerchief she meandered into the dark living room and sank onto the lumpy sofa. The hours after Kyle's bedtime were hers to spend as she wished, and she often used them to review the day and plan the next. Unlike some of her friends, she reveled in the quiet, enjoying every creak her house made because it was hers, thanks to hard work and sacrifice.

Tonight, however, the memories that Peter Caldwell had stirred, the memories she'd repressed for ten years, refused to remain in the background. . .

'You've got to help me, Lib,' Elaine announced before she burst into tears. 'I'm pregnant.'

Libby stared at her elder sister. 'You're *what*?'

'I'm—'

'Never mind. I heard you the first time.' Libby sank onto the desk chair. Her dorm room-mate had made the same announcement several days earlier and now Libby felt as if she were part of an epidemic. 'How did it happen?'

Elaine started to speak, but Libby forestalled her with a wave. 'Never mind the details—I'm a biology major. Forget I asked.' She crossed her arms. 'Who's the father?'

'Bryce Caldwell.'

The surname captured Libby's attention. 'Bryce Caldwell of Caldwell Industries?'

Elaine nodded as she plucked at a loose thread on the white chenille bedspread.

'Have you told him?'

Nodding, Elaine wiped her eyes.

'What did he say?'

Elaine drew a deep breath. 'He said a lot of things, but mainly that he won't be trapped into marriage. If I name him as the father or sue him for child support his family will fight for custody. With their high-powered attorneys, I won't win.'

Libby shook her head. 'How *did* you meet this guy?'

Elaine colored. 'At the mall. He literally ran into me. After he picked me off the floor he bought me a soft drink. Gosh, Lib. He was so charming.'

'I'll bet.' Sarcasm dripped from her words.

'He was,' Elaine insisted. 'Once he said his name I knew I wouldn't hold his interest so. . .' she winced '. . .I pretended I was you.'

'What?'

Elaine nodded. 'I told him I was a pre-med student at KU on a full scholarship. He was impressed—a lot more so than if I'd admitted to being a cashier at Wal-Mart.

'Anyway, things progressed and now I'm pregnant.' Elaine paused. 'I thought he loved me like I loved him, but I was obviously wrong.' She smiled through her tears. 'That'll teach me to think, won't it, Sis?'

Libby crossed the room. She sat beside her sister and hugged her. 'You're too trusting, that's all. Don't worry, though. Everything will work out.'

The telephone rang and Libby grabbed the receiver.

'You have a visitor, Ms Brown,' the girl at the reception desk reported. She lowered her voice and continued. 'If I were you I wouldn't keep this guy waiting. Someone will steal him from under your nose.'

'Who is he?'

'Beats me, but you'd better get down here before all the girls end up at Student Health for whiplash.'

'Be right there.' Libby hung up. 'Someone's down-stairs, waiting to see me. I'll see who it is and what he wants so don't go away.'

She rushed down the two flights of stairs, slowing to a sedate walk before entering the lobby. The dorm's student receptionist pointed toward the visitor as he paced the floor. Not recognizing him, Libby approached—feeling surprised, curious, and somewhat awed that this good-looking, self-possessed man wanted to see *her*.

'Hello. I'm—'

He swung around. 'Miss Brown?'

She nodded. He appeared even more handsome up close.

'I'm Peter Caldwell.'

Recognizing the surname, it was clear how Elaine had been bowled over by Bryce's attention. Her smile died.

He raised one sardonic eyebrow. 'Did you think I was Bryce?'

'Actually, I—'

'I'm surprised you'd make that mistake, especially after knowing Bryce in the biblical sense.'

'Why did you come?' Now that she had pulled her wits together, she didn't care if she sounded rude.

'Bryce asked if I would.'

She couldn't restrain her sarcasm. 'To negotiate a reconciliation, perhaps?'

He glanced away. 'No.'

Crossing her arms, she rephrased her question. 'Then why are you here?'

'To find out what you intend to do.'

'I haven't decided,' she said, testing his response.

Peter pulled a long white envelope out of his wool blazer's inner breast pocket and held it out. 'This con-tains the name of a physician who will help you. His services won't cost you a dime if you give him the letter inside.'

'How thoughtful,' she said with scorn, refusing the envelope. 'I assume this person specializes in abortions?'

At least he had the grace to look uncomfortable. 'He can also arrange an adoption, if you'd prefer.'

'And if I choose not to avail myself of your— Bryce's—generosity?'

Peter's gaze held hers under a mesmerizing spell. 'You're an intelligent woman with a promising future, or so I've been told. It wouldn't be in your best interests to throw away this opportunity to start over. I believe my cousin has made it clear that marriage and long-term support is out of the question.'

'Oh, definitely. Now that he's had his fun he's off to greener pastures.'

'He has plans for his life.'

'I do, too.'

His eyes narrowed. 'Then I suggest you accept and be satisfied with the help Bryce is willing to give.'

Thinking of her heartbroken sister, she tried a different approach. 'Won't you at least ask him to reconsider—?'

'Bryce's made his decision. Accept it.'

'So you condone what he's doing?'

'You wouldn't be the first girl who tried to trap a man, especially a wealthy one.'

Libby seethed. '*Real* men don't lead women on.'

Peter's jaw squared and his pulse visibly throbbed in his temple. It obviously took a great deal of effort on his part to hold back his comment.

Instead, he grabbed her wrist in a vise-like grip. Using his other hand, he closed her fingers around the envelope which retained his body heat. 'I won't be in touch,

Miss Brown, but I hope you'll make the right decision. One you won't regret in the long run. . .'

The furnace whirred to life, startling Libby out of the past and into the present.

She'd never accepted ultimatums well, although she had followed Peter's final piece of advice. She and Elaine had made the only decision they could live with—the only one they wouldn't regret.

In spite of opposition from her parents, Elaine had wanted her baby. Afraid that the Caldwells would create problems if Elaine didn't appear at the doctor's office, Libby had given the letter to her grateful room-mate.

Meanwhile, she'd finished her first year of college and moved to Quincy, Illinois, where their uncle lived and where Kyle had been born.

Throughout the following months Libby had taken perverse pleasure in knowing they had circumvented Bryce Caldwell's scheme. Deep down, however, she'd feared the possibility that she'd not covered their tracks. It had taken many months before the nightmares of Peter demanding Bryce's son had stopped.

Elaine herself, however, had plotted a deeper deception which hadn't been revealed until after her death from pneumonia.

She had used Elizabeth's name on the birth certificate. Elizabeth Brown, not Elaine, was recorded as the mother. Even the signature matched Libby's.

Libby refused to think of the legal tangles Elaine had created—forgery came to mind—but she couldn't fault her sister's actions. In fact, she was glad Elaine had taken the extra steps to protect her son.

Just as Libby would move heaven and earth to shield Kyle from the Caldwells.

She sighed. Her plan to avoid Peter Caldwell had

developed a new twist. Steering clear of him at the hospital was challenging in itself. Keeping out of his way after she'd promised to include Samantha in their Christmas preparations was nearly impossible.

But one way or another she would. She had no choice.

Peter stacked the report he'd been studying and stuffed it in his briefcase. Leaning against the sofa cushions, he propped his feet on the coffee-table and stared at the saucer containing remnants of cherry pie filling.

He'd wondered who the attractive and intriguing woman on the elevator had been—Eldon hadn't known. How fortunate to have her appear on his doorstep, revealing her identity so easily. Her proximity as neighbor provided an added bonus.

He grinned. His decision to join a medical practice in Belleville was turning out to be the best one he'd made in a long time.

# CHAPTER THREE

'DON'T forget to see your doctor in about ten days,' Libby reminded Ralph. 'He'll take the cast off your leg, remove the stitches, then recast for another five weeks.'

'I won't,' Ralph grumbled, clearly annoyed by the inconvenience.

She glanced at the page of hospital-release instructions. Satisfied she'd covered every one, she signed the designated line at the bottom and handed the form to Ralph.

'The home health nurse will stop by every day to check on you, help with a bath and whatever else you need. The agency scheduled your visit for ten a.m., but don't be surprised if she's running late.'

'Hmm. You'd think they'd show up on time.'

'If you don't like these arrangements I can always contact your son.'

'He and his wife would just put me in a nursing home, and I'm *not* going.'

'If you don't co-operate with the visiting nurse you may not have a choice,' Libby warned. 'They're in too much demand to put up with irascible patients.'

He exhaled a drawn-out breath. 'I'll behave.'

'And don't forget Sylvia will keep you company for a few hours each afternoon, too.'

'Goody.'

Libby laughed at his glum expression. 'Admit it. The highlight of your day is arguing with her.'

The corners of his mouth curved ever so slightly. 'Maybe.'

'Why *do* you two antagonize each other?'

'Because she—'

Sylvia breezed in, smiling. 'Hello, hello. Well, Ralph, are you ready to blow this joint?'

'Yeah, but I don't see why *you* have to drive me home.'

'Because no one else will, you old coot. Now hush up and let's get going.'

His eyes narrowed. 'And how in the world are you going to get me out of the car and inside my house? You can't lift anything heavier than your checkbook.'

'I knew you were jealous of the money my husband left me,' she said triumphantly. 'This just proves it.'

'Does not.'

Libby broke in, wondering if it had been wise for Sylvia to provide transportation. 'How *will* you get Ralph home?'

Sylvia straightened her shoulders. 'I've enlisted some of the fellows from the senior center. They're waiting for us at the house now.'

A picture of several elderly men helping another out of the car and into a wheelchair seemed almost frightening. Libby turned to Ralph. 'Maybe you should wait until I can be there to help.'

'Nonsense.' Sylvia waved one age-spotted hand. 'We'll be fine. No one will drop Ralph unless he continues to act like a horse's posterior.'

Ralph glared at Sylvia, his mouth pinched, but mercifully he remained silent.

Libby wheeled Ralph toward the elevator and Sylvia walked alongside, carrying Ralph's evergreen and his bag of personal articles.

Luckily, the elevator trip went without a hitch and soon they'd installed Ralph in Sylvia's car.

'I'll check in on you when I get home,' Libby told

him before she slammed the door closed.

'Hope so,' he muttered. 'No telling what this harridan will do to me without witnesses.'

Sylvia struck a pose and fluffed her platinum-blonde hair. 'Wish all you want, Ralph Upton.'

Ralph's jaw dropped. Stifling her own grin, Libby shook her head in a resigned gesture. 'See you two later.'

Once they'd driven away she returned to her unit. Knowing Ira Kendrick was also scheduled to leave, she stopped by his room. There she found one of her colleagues and several staff from the nursing home collecting his few possessions.

'Take care,' she said, patting his shoulder. 'No wheelchair races for a while.'

Ira grinned, his sparse gray hair slicked down. 'I'll wait for a few weeks.'

'I'll miss you,' she said.

'I never turn away visitors. Bring your son and you can meet my Ella.'

'It's a date.'

'Time to go, Mr Kendrick,' one of the home's attendants said.

He gave Libby a jaunty wave. 'Don't forget,' he called over his shoulder as his entourage wheeled him down the hallway.

Before she could turn away Ann waved her forward. 'ER has a new admission for us. Are you available to run down and get her?'

'Sure. What's the problem?'

'A twenty-six-year-old female with fever and lower back pain. I'll notify them you're on your way.'

Libby took the stairs and arrived in the emergency room a few minutes later. Daryl, a nurse-practitioner, and Peter Caldwell were seated at the nurses' station.

Daryl was entering data into a computer terminal while Peter had the telephone receiver to his ear.

As she approached the desk Daryl glanced up and gratitude crossed his fortyish features. 'Thanks for helping us out,' he said, rising to lead the way to a cubicle. 'Your patient's name is Kathy Sanders. The lab results just arrived. She's anemic with eight grams of hemoglobin, her white count is slightly elevated at twelve thousand and her urine tests show definite abnormalities—protein, hemoglobin, bacteria, white cells and casts.'

Since urine was normally sterile and didn't have the aforementioned elements present, the report caught her attention. 'Kidney or bladder infection?'

'Ms Sanders was treated with an antibiotic several weeks ago but, from the report, her condition hasn't improved. Now her kidney function tests, namely the urea nitrogen, are slightly elevated. With protein and casts spilling into the urine, she's got major problems. Probably bleeding somewhere, too.'

Daryl pushed open the door and strode to the head of the gurney. 'Kathy? Libby will take you upstairs and find you a real bed.'

'I'm ready.' The young woman pressed a hand to her abdomen and grimaced. Her slim body barely made a lump underneath the white sheet, which matched the color of her face. Her mouse-brown hair was limp; lines etched her features and shadows appeared under her eyes.

He spoke to the girl—obviously a younger relative— hovering nearby. 'Why don't you get a cup of coffee while we make your sister comfortable? We'll be taking her to—' He glanced at Libby.

'Room four-eleven,' she supplied. 'Give us about twenty minutes.'

The blonde patted Kathy's fine-boned hand. 'See you later. I won't go far.'

The picture reminded Libby of the time when she'd been in the same situation with Elaine. She looked away, surprised to feel the pain so acutely after all this time.

Daryl pushed the trolley forward while Libby guided her end through the doorway. To her surprise, Peter fell into step beside them and laid the chart near Kathy's feet.

'I'll help,' Peter told Daryl, edging his way into the nurse-practitioner's position. His gray trousers, long-sleeved maroon shirt and geometric-print tie gave him a distinguished appearance. The stethoscope around his neck added to the picture that he wasn't an ordinary hospital employee.

'Are you sure?' Daryl asked, clearly anxious to be relieved of this duty in favor of the pressing obligations in his own department yet uncertain about enlisting a physician for such lowly work.

'I'm going up, anyway. We can handle a gurney, can't we, Libby?'

'Yes, but—'

'Great. I owe you one.' With that, Daryl returned to the desk and Peter pushed the patient through the corridors toward the restricted-use elevators.

Libby hurried to keep pace with his long strides. 'I can manage on my own.'

'Probably. But I'd like to talk to you about something.'

Imagining the worst, she peered into his face, but his expression was placid and gave her no clue as to what the discussion involved. She swallowed and pretended nonchalance. 'Oh?'

He motioned to the patient with a tilt of his head.

'Later.' Before she could quiz him further they'd rounded the corner and found the elevator waiting with its doors wide open.

After wheeling Kathy inside Libby depressed the fourth floor button. As the doors slid shut he moved next to her and whispered, 'I can manage if you'd rather walk.'

'I'm fine.' One of his eyebrows lifted and she added, 'Really.'

They arrived at their destination without any unnecessary stops on the floors in between. Once Kathy had been transferred to a bed Peter pulled Libby aside. 'Start an IV. The lab collected the blood cultures downstairs so infuse the broad-spectrum antibiotics as soon as you receive the medication from Pharmacy. I've written the specifics in the chart. Monitor her closely.'

'I will.'

Libby began the flurry of activity that came with a hospital admission—taking vital signs and a detailed patient history, as well as implementing the doctor's orders. A nurse from the IV therapy team arrived several minutes later to start the intravenous fluid line.

Kathy's sister stood in the doorway. 'May I come in?'

'Sure can,' Libby answered cheerfully. 'We're finished for the moment.' The other RN left while Libby disposed of the used equipment, speaking while she did so. 'You must be Becky. Are you older or younger?'

'Younger.' Becky motioned Libby aside. 'Kathy's the only family I have. Will she be OK?'

Struck by how the situation seemed to be an exact replay of her own, Libby empathized. 'We're doing all we can.'

'I've never heard of Dr Caldwell before. Is he any good?' Judging from Becky's tone, she wanted an assurance from someone who was in a position to evaluate his skill.

Patient confidence was important to recovery so Libby repeated the cafeteria gossip. 'He's new in town, but I hear he's thorough. Your sister's in good hands.'

The relief on Becky's face sent a shaft of worry through Libby. If Peter wasn't the physician she'd declared him to be she'd meddle where she shouldn't and either demand he transfer Kathy to another facility or encourage Becky to make the arrangements.

'If you need anything or have questions just pull the cord. I'll be right outside.'

Leaving Kathy in her sister's company, Libby returned to the nurses' station to complete her own records.

Movement out of the corner of one eye caught her attention and an instant later Peter sank into the chair beside hers. His masculine fragrance drifted in her direction, providing a pleasant contrast to the usual hospital odors. The scent wrought total havoc with her professional composure.

How ridiculous, she scolded herself. Rubbing her nose, she forced her thoughts onto business.

'Possible septicemia,' she said in a low voice. 'The poor thing has a serious preliminary diagnosis.'

'I hope I'm wrong, but. . .' He shrugged. 'We'll know more after the microbiology reports come in.'

Libby stared at the chart in front of her, gathering courage to mention her concerns. 'Her sister asked for my opinion about you.'

'What did you tell her?'

She swiveled her chair to face him. 'I told her you were thorough and that Kathy was in good hands.'

His mouth curled into a small smile. 'Thanks for the vote of confidence.'

Leaning forward, she hardened her voice. 'I hope you live up to that glowing recommendation.'

'You don't think I will, do you?'

She turned away to avoid his sharp gaze. 'If her condition is beyond your expertise please transfer her to another facility.'

He squared his jaw and the pulse in his temple throbbed. 'Aren't you being presumptuous, *Nurse* Brown? I could turn you in for insubordination.'

'You could,' she admitted.

'If you try to intimidate all the doctors I'm surprised you're still employed.'

'I don't,' she answered stiffly. 'But I have my reasons for being so vocal.'

'Care to enlighten me?'

'No.' Although it would be a blot on her perfect record, she didn't care if her comments earned her a counseling memo. Kathy deserved the best and Libby would do whatever she could to ensure that her patient received it.

The lines of controlled fury on his face softened. 'I assume this scenario hits close to home in some way.'

His insight surprised her. 'It does,' she said, her voice hoarse.

'In that case, I won't take your comments personally. This time.'

For a few seconds silence fell between them. When Peter broke the quiet it was as if their tense exchange had never happened.

'She's about your age, isn't she?'

'Yes, although I'm a year older. What's her prognosis?' Having made her point, she, too, was willing to put their confrontation behind her.

His forehead wrinkled in thought. 'Fair, depending on how she responds to treatment.'

For a split second Libby wondered what she'd do if she walked in Kathy Sanders's shoes. Where would Kyle go? Her parents were dead, her aunt and uncle were in their seventies and Libby didn't consider their flighty daughter a suitable candidate to raise her son. Maybe it was time she planned for such a possibility—one never knew what twists and turns lay in the future.

'Hey, don't look like it's the end of the world,' he said. 'I've had patients in worse shape pull through.'

His comment interrupted her introspection and she managed a smile. 'Of course. There's always hope.'

He rested one elbow on the table. 'Can we talk for a minute?'

Her breath seemed to catch in her throat. 'About what?'

'I'm in a dilemma of sorts. Mrs Bridges doesn't drive and I can't always get away from the clinic or the hospital to take Samantha home. Could she car-pool with you?'

The band around her chest loosened. 'I'd be happy to give her a ride. If I'm working late the lady next door, Sylvia Posy, takes over as chauffeur.'

'Do you think she'd mind dropping Sam by our house?'

'Not at all. Sylvia adores children.'

'Then it's settled. For my part, I'll take the two of them to school every morning.'

'That isn't necessary,' she answered quickly. 'Your place isn't out of our way so there's no favor to return. You don't need to bother.' The less contact between Kyle and Peter the better. Just because Peter hadn't recognized her or become suspicious didn't mean she could press her luck. Especially since her luck had a propensity for being bad.

'It isn't a bother. Your house isn't out of our way either.'

In Libby's mind, his suggestion was trouble with a capital T. 'Thanks for the offer, but I hate to change our routine. If something comes up I'll let you know.' The situation would have to be dire before she asked for his assistance, and even then she probably wouldn't.

'I don't want to impose.' His dark gaze remained on her face. 'Surely we can work out a less one-sided arrangement.'

'I'm not complaining. I'm happy to help out a new neighbor.' She pretended to study the chart in front of her.

'Speaking of being neighbors, I trust your rule about Kyle associating with strangers no longer applies to us?'

Now she knew what the expression 'between a rock and a hard place' meant. 'I guess not.'

A satisfied smile appeared on his face. He'd obviously not noticed how she'd forced the words from her mouth. 'We'd like Kyle to go swimming with us at the spa's pool some afternoon. You're welcome, too.'

An image of a well-formed male rising out of the water, droplets clinging to his skin, made her mouth dry. 'We're not members.'

'You'll be our guests.'

'Kyle doesn't swim very well.'

'I'm a certified Red Cross instructor,' he continued. 'I'll be happy to work with him.'

Tenacious. Peter Caldwell had more than his fair share of the trait. If Bryce had hammered at Elaine so convincingly no wonder her sister—and any other starry-eyed female—had caved in to his coercion.

'I'm afraid our Saturdays and Sundays will be busy for a while. Christmas, you know.'

Judging from his expression, he thought her excuse

flimsy. To a certain extent it was. She'd always given Kyle the opportunity to spend time with his pals on the weekends.

'If you find a few free hours, or if you'd like Kyle out of your hair to shop for his presents, he's welcome at our place.'

Suspicion rose. 'Have you made the same offer to Samantha's other school friends?'

He appeared sheepish. 'I'm afraid not.'

'Then why *my* son?'

He leaned back in his chair and held his hands together so that only his fingertips touched. 'I'm not sure. Have you ever met someone with whom you felt an instant kinship, a special bond?'

Libby clenched her teeth and stiffened. Fear filled her mouth and she struggled to swallow its bitter taste. Keeping her gaze fixed on his eyes, she forced herself to breathe evenly and remain calm.

'I've felt that with Kyle,' he said. 'He's a good kid. You've done an excellent job in raising him.'

'Thank you,' she whispered.

'You two must have been alone for a long time.'

She glanced away and rubbed suddenly sweaty palms on her uniform trousers. 'Yes, we have.'

'I could tell. You're independent.'

Unsure if she was being derided or complimented, she studied his face. 'Shouldn't I be?'

The light above room four-sixteen blinked on with an audible click. At the same time his pager bleeped. She pushed the telephone toward him and rose, thankful for the interruption.

Talking to Peter about her past was the last thing on earth she wanted to do.

Eldon Hanover motioned Peter into his plush administrator's office. 'Thanks for studying the past two quarters' financial statements. If anyone could find some angle I've missed I knew you would. Having a physician on board who also has a degree in business administration is a definite plus, especially since that physician is an old friend.'

Peter tossed a cream-colored folder onto Eldon's desk before he sat in one of the two padded wing chairs across from his college classmate. 'Thanks for the compliment, but I'm afraid you were right.'

Eldon's expression turned serious. 'You couldn't find any other way to solve our problem either.'

'To be blunt, you're losing money,' Peter said. 'Your cost containment measures have worked to a certain degree, but it's not enough.'

'I hate to lay people off,' Eldon admitted. 'The hospital is one of the largest employers in this area.'

'If you don't adjust your expenses to fit your income you won't have a choice. From a medical perspective, however, you can't sacrifice patient care for the sake of a few dollars. There's a fine line to walk, a delicate balance to be achieved. It won't be easy.'

Eldon drew a deep breath. 'I know, which is why I asked you to review our reports. I'd hoped you'd see more options than I did.'

'If you recruit a few more physicians, convince more patients to use the facilities here rather than go elsewhere, you shouldn't have to resort to such drastic measures.'

'In the meantime, though. . .'

'In the meantime, grit your teeth and tighten your belt.'

'I'll start by announcing a hiring freeze. Those who resign or retire won't be replaced.'

'Eliminating overtime, freezing salaries, that sort of

thing should also help. If not, your cuts will have to go deeper.'

Eldon pressed his mouth into a hard line. 'I'll notify the personnel department to prepare a seniority list in case we have to use it. Thanks for your input and for verifying my conclusions.'

'My pleasure. It's been a long time since I analyzed financial information. Keep something in mind, though. If I see patients receiving shabby care I'll lead the opposition.'

Eldon made a face, then laughed. 'Don't remind me. I know how hard you are to fight against and win.' He relaxed in his chair. 'Are you settled in your home? Does your daughter like her school?'

Peter followed the subject switch, grinning as he recalled Samantha's exuberance each morning. 'She loves it.' His smile died. 'She's starting to get into this Christmas thing, and I'm not sure I'm ready.'

'It's been a few years, hasn't it?'

'Four,' Peter corrected. 'I've treated the holiday like any other day for a long time. The decorations, parties and all the other trappings of the season don't bring back pleasant memories.' Christmas was supposed to be a time of peace and goodwill, not betrayal—and certainly not by his own wife.

'Then you need to associate new things, *enjoyable* things, with Christmas. God knows it's long overdue.'

'Maybe you're right,' Peter said, thinking of Libby and Kyle and the city's contest.

'It shouldn't be too difficult.' Eldon winked. 'Every eligible woman in the hospital would literally kill for a date with you.'

'I know.' Peter gave his friend a disgusted look. 'I feel like I'm in the middle of a shark feeding frenzy. I can always tell who's on the prowl for a husband. Today

I had one woman stop me in the cafeteria and offer to buy my lunch. And serve it to me.' He grimaced.

'You always were good with the ladies. You and your cousin both. How's Bryce doing, by the way?'

'Fine. He's Vice-President of Caldwell Industries now. Married; three children, all girls. I usually see him when we go back to Lawrence for Christmas.'

'Maybe you'll have someone special to introduce to your parents this year.'

'I doubt it.' Yet he couldn't dispel the image of Libby fearlessly cautioning him about Kathy Sanders. She was the only unattached female he'd met who didn't appear to be consumed with a desire to end his bachelorhood.

'It's got to be hard, raising a daughter alone.'

Peter shrugged. 'I have a housekeeper.'

'It's not the same. I'd hate to think of dealing with my girls if Tonya wasn't around.'

A mental picture of Libby appeared. 'Actually, one of my neighbors is rather intriguing.'

'Ah,' Eldon said, knowingly. 'I see that smile.'

Peter's grin grew broader. 'Sammie thinks she's wonderful. Her name is Libby Brown and she's a nurse here at St Nick's.'

Eldon's eyes narrowed. 'Libby Brown,' he mused aloud. 'Doesn't ring a bell.'

'Remember the woman who was almost sick in the elevator yesterday? About five feet six, long curly hair, big eyes, pretty.'

'Oh, yeah. I think she was in the last crop of nursing graduates we hired.'

The information made her outburst over his patient more interesting. Even if the case had touched a sore spot why would Libby risk a reprimand?

Eldon's stare became intense. 'Interested in her?'

Peter shrugged. 'She and her son are my neighbors.

In fact, Libby is the only single woman who hasn't looked at me like I'm an answer to her prayer. She's polite, friendly to a point, although definitely reserved.'

'And your daughter likes her?'

'That's an understatement,' Peter said wryly. 'Since Libby invited Sam to help prepare for Christmas Sam hasn't talked about anything else.'

'How convenient. You wouldn't have to worry about Sam having a wicked stepmother.'

'True.'

'On the other hand, she could be using Sam to get close to you.'

Peter recalled how uncomfortable she usually seemed in his presence. 'I don't think so.'

'I have an idea.' Eldon reached for the phone and punched three buttons before he spoke into the receiver. 'Mrs Fitzgerald? Could you come in, please?'

He hung up. 'My secretary has been here for ages and knows everyone and everything. I'll bet she can supply whatever information you want.' He winked. 'Naturally, this is only to determine if Libby would be a suitable influence on your daughter.'

Peter smiled.

The door opened and a well-dressed woman in her late fifties entered. 'You asked for me, Mr Hanover?'

'Do you know a Libby Brown? Dr Caldwell is her neighbor and she has a son close to his daughter's age. Since they'll be playing together. . .'

Mrs Fitzgerald addressed Peter. 'Libby's a wonderful nurse and absolutely dotes on her little boy. In fact, she started here at St Nick's several years ago after taking a medication aide course. After that she worked on her nursing degree, although it took her longer than most because she was a part-time student.

'She graduated last spring and we hired her for the

floating nurse pool. It's technically not a full-time position, but she's one of the few who work a full forty-hour
week. Nurse managers ask for her by name.'

Eldon appeared triumphant. 'What did I tell you?'
he boasted. 'Mrs Fitzgerald, you have a phenomenal
memory. Are you sure I can't talk you out of your
retirement plans?'

She smiled. 'Sorry.'

Peter filed the information away, certain he could use
what he'd learned. 'Is she widowed or divorced?'

A furrow appeared on Mrs Fitzgerald's brow and her
eyes narrowed, apparently in thought. 'I'm not sure. I
believe she moved here while her child was still a
toddler, and there wasn't a Mr Brown then. Whatever
happened in her personal life was obviously during her
pre-Belleville days.'

'Thanks,' Peter said.

'You're welcome.'

Peter's pager bleeped again. An extension number
appeared on the small screen. 'Four-one-five,' he read
aloud. 'That's fourth floor, isn't it?'

Eldon nodded. 'Four north.' He scooted the phone
on his desk forward.

Peter rose, realizing it was Libby's unit. 'No, thanks.
I'll run up there instead. It probably concerns my new
admission.'

His rush to the fourth floor was a combination of
concern for his newest patient and excitement at the
prospect of talking to Libby again. He glanced at his
watch. It had only been thirty minutes since he'd seen
either of them.

'I'm concerned about Kathy,' Libby told him as soon
as he strode into the nurses' station. 'She's bleeding
around her IV site.'

Her observation brought a new condition to mind,

one that he'd hoped wouldn't come to pass. 'Order a fibrinogen level and a test for fibrin degradation products, stat.'

Immediately Libby reached for the telephone. A few moments later she covered the mouthpiece with her hand. 'Can the lab use the specimen they collected in ER an hour ago?'

'Yes.'

She spoke into the receiver again, then hung up. 'We should have the results in about fifteen minutes.'

'Good.' Mentally he revised his diagnosis.

She spoke in a low voice. 'What's wrong with her?'

'I'd bet money that she has DIC, disseminated intravascular coagulation,' he said grimly.

'When the blood clots in the body, right?'

'That's a simplified explanation. More specifically, the blood-clotting mechanisms—platelets, clotting factors, fibrinogen—become overstimulated because of a disease or injury. The factors and fibrinogen are used up to form fibrin clots, which is why the coagulation times are prolonged.

'Meanwhile, the body tries to dissolve the fibrin material, and those degradation products appear in the plasma as well. A vicious cycle starts because these FDPs, as they're called, interfere with platelet function and as a result more bleeding occurs.'

'So she has blood in the urine.'

'Exactly. Since the body's ability to dissolve the clots can't keep up with the demand, the fibrin is deposited in the veins and capillaries. And since the kidney functions as a blood filter—'

'It becomes clogged.'

'In a manner of speaking. Consequently, if left untreated, kidney damage results.'

Libby's face blanched. 'But why did it start? I thought

this condition was associated with obstetric patients who retained a dead fetus. She's not pregnant.'

'It's also associated with certain malignancies and infections. In the latter case, gram-negative organisms like *E. coli* are usually involved, although not always. I had a case where the causative agent was *Staph aureus*.

'In any case,' he finished, 'since Kathy's running a fever, I'm guessing her blood cultures will be positive.'

'Then antibiotics will take care of it.' Her shoulders sagged with apparent relief.

'If we deal successfully with the underlying cause, the DIC should resolve itself.'

Her eyes narrowed. 'What do you mean "should"?'

'The long-term outlook depends on how badly her kidneys are affected. Some patients recover—some, unfortunately, don't.' Peter hated to see the dismay on her face, but he couldn't allow false hope. Time would tell.

'What about a transplant?'

'It's possible, but let's not get ahead of ourselves. At this point the diagnosis isn't confirmed.'

The printer whirred to life a few feet away. Libby jumped to her feet. 'Maybe those are her results now.' She walked to the machine and lifted the papers from the bin. After glancing at the name she handed them to Peter. 'Perfect timing.'

He scanned the documents. The numbers fitted the pattern he'd expected.

'Well?'

'Just as I thought, although I wish I'd been wrong.' He rose, flexing his shoulders. 'I'm not sure where I'll be for the next few hours so page me if you notice any change.'

'I will.'

He turned to go, then stopped. 'Libby?'

She glanced up, her pen poised over the page and her expression expectant. 'Yes?'

'Thanks for being so observant.'

Her face became pink. 'Just doing my job.'

Peter spent the next hour touring the various hospital departments, familiarizing himself with the layout of the facility. At three o'clock he left ICU. On impulse, he bypassed the bank of elevators in favor of the stairs.

As he swung the door open he saw Libby a few steps above him. Grinning, he waited for her to descend, then matched his pace to hers. 'Going home?'

Her coat was buttoned all the way to her throat. 'Yes.' She glanced at him. 'Is the elevator broken?'

'No, but I felt like stretching my legs.' In truth, he'd only made that decision in the last few moments. Trying to run into Libby was certain to improve his cardio-vascular system.

An idea which had been simmering all afternoon in the back of his mind hit him again full strength.

'I'm looking for an office nurse.'

She stopped abruptly. 'Isn't Dr Greenburg's nurse staying?'

He shook his head. 'Her husband's been bitten by the traveling bug and now she wants to quit.'

'Oh.' She walked on. 'If I hear of anyone who wants a job I'll steer them in your direction.'

'Actually, I already have someone in mind.' He hesitated. He'd reached the point of no return. 'Would you be interested?'

# CHAPTER FOUR

LIBBY blinked and froze in mid-stride. 'Me? You want *me* to be your office nurse?'

Peter grinned. 'Yes, you.'

'Why?'

'Why not?' he countered.

She chewed on her lower lip. She could think of several reasons, none of which she'd divulge. Instead, she mentioned what she thought would be a legitimate excuse.

'I prefer the hustle and bustle of acute care.'

'It *is* a tough decision. You'd exchange being on your feet all day, working short of staff and covering weekends and holidays for regular hours and a slower, more flexible pace.'

She caught his dry humor. 'The hospital pays well.'

'I'll match your salary.'

Her jaw dropped in surprise. 'You're kidding!'

'No.'

He was offering the job of her dreams, and yet... 'Any nurse would jump at your offer—'

He held her gaze. 'But not you?'

She shrugged. 'Thanks for thinking of me, though.'

'What kind of seniority do you have at St Nick's?'

'Practically none. I've only been in a registered nurse's position since May.'

'Layoffs are a very real possibility.'

'Strictly rumor.' She turned and hurried down the second flight.

For the next few minutes she concentrated on each

step until at last she reached the door to the ground floor lobby.

Without warning, his arm shot out and he held the door closed. He'd cut off her means of escape. 'It's not rumor.'

'How can you be so sure?' Even as she spoke she knew the answer.

'Eldon is an old friend of mine. In fact, we discussed the probability only a few hours ago.'

Warily she asked, 'Why tell me?'

One corner of his mouth turned upward. 'Do you realize you're always asking me why? My own daughter doesn't ask that question as often as you do.'

She folded her arms. 'I want to understand your motives. People usually don't do something for nothing.'

'I'm telling you so you'll keep your eyes open for opportunities.'

'Why are you so interested in whether I have a job or not?'

'Because I care what happens to you,' he said simply.

Libby's jaw went slack. She couldn't have been more surprised if he'd kissed her.

'I care because Sam likes you and because I think Kyle's a neat kid.' He rubbed the back of his neck. 'Maybe it's because you're vivacious and mysterious—'

Oh, God. He thought she was *mysterious*. 'My life's an open book,' she lied.

'I feel as if I should know you.'

Her heart fluttered. 'Everyone has a twin or so I've been told.'

'You know something else? I admire you.'

She forgot to breathe. 'You. . .do?'

'You've accomplished so much on your own—

raising a child, obtaining your education, holding down a job in the process. It couldn't have been easy.'

Her eyes burned and she blinked rapidly. Once again he'd surprised her with his compassion. 'Why be impressed? There are probably more single parents than not. You were—are—in the same situation.'

He shook his head. 'My parents and our hired house-keepers saw Sam more than I did. The years of medical training don't allow for much of a family life. In any event, I'd like to help you now.'

*Be grateful and accept the help Bryce can give you.* The words echoed from the past as clearly as if he'd spoken them. He'd paraphrased the sentence and substituted his name for his cousin's, but the meaning was identical. She bristled.

'Thanks,' she said, her tone cool, 'but I don't need your—or anyone else's—help.' My sister needed it ten years ago, she cried out inside.

'You are the most stubborn woman I've ever met,' he said, sounding exasperated.

'I'll take that as a compliment.'

'It's my turn for a question. Are you this unco-operative with everyone, or just me?'

'I prefer to rely on myself.' Understanding how a trapped animal felt, she pointed to the door. 'May I go?'

Peter didn't move. 'Your ex really did a number on you, didn't he?'

Without thinking, she snapped, 'I've never been married.' Her comment hung in the air and she regretted her loss of control.

'Ah-h. Left you high and dry, so to speak.'

How could she have let her marital status slip into the conversation? Now he had another clue. She could only hope the rest of her past would remain an unsolved mystery.

'Yes, but. . .' she swallowed hard '. . .no one knows.'

'Don't worry. I've already forgotten.'

His kindness and gentle tone caught her off guard. Her voice quivered. 'Please open the door.'

As if he sensed she was near her breaking point, he stepped aside and tugged on the door.

Libby rushed through the portal. Reaching the other side, she stopped and turned to face him. 'Thanks again for the offer, but I can't accept.'

'I won't make a decision for another week or so. If you change your mind. . .' His voice died.

She pressed her mouth into a semblance of a smile, then fled. Truthfully, she would have loved the job. Everything about it—the hours, the salary, the pace—sounded perfect, and if anyone else had made the same proposition she would have jumped at the chance.

The prospect of losing her position was worrisome, but working in Peter Caldwell's employ was defying fate. She wasn't brave enough to do so.

Peter stood on Libby's porch two days later, his shoulders hunched against the cold—her pie plate in hand. He hadn't seen her since they'd talked in the stairwell and he wondered what kind of reception he'd receive.

It couldn't be too bad, he thought. Libby had allowed Sam to participate in a cookie-baking project after school.

The door flung open and Libby stepped aside. 'Hi,' she said, sounding breathless. 'Won't you come in? The time ran away from us. I didn't intend to keep Sam so long.'

Peter walked in, hearing children's Christmas songs in the background. 'I wasn't worried but I thought I'd check on you guys.' He sniffed the air laden with the scent of freshly baked cookies. 'Pure ambrosia. Like the pie.'

Libby blushed. 'I hope they taste as good as they smell,' she said, leading the way into the kitchen.

He followed, noticing the flour dusting Libby's face and clothing and the smears of frosting on one cheek. Her figure in a hospital uniform was delightful, but to see her in jeans—what an unexpected pleasure.

The denim molded itself to her hips and the soft shirt she wore clung to her curves. She'd clipped her hair in a ponytail high on her head and the curly strands hung down to her nape. The tall column of her neck made his fingers itch. He imagined how soft her skin would feel.

What a shame she'd refused his invitation to go swimming. He'd love to see her in a suit, her lithe body shimmering from the jewel-like qualities of water.

He caught sight of his daughter and forced his mind off Libby's form. 'How's the baking business, Sammie?'

His daughter stood on a dinette chair, looking more disheveled than Libby. The gingham apron wrapped around her waist was entirely white, and as she moved a cloud of flour drifted to the floor.

'Real good, Daddy. Come see.'

He peered over her shoulder. Christmas tree-shaped sugar cookies covered the baking sheet. Some were crooked, some had a few boughs missing and some carried a distinct thumbprint.

'Aren't they just beautiful?' Sam crooned, exaggerating her pronunciation.

Kyle snickered.

'They'll be fancier after we frost them,' Libby said, sending an obvious warning look toward her son before she slid the pan into the oven.

'Can I take one home for Mrs Bridges?'

Libby smiled. 'You may take half of them.'

Sam clapped her hands, raising another cloud of flour. 'All right!' Her exuberance faded and a frown appeared. 'Do we have to go now?'

'You don't want to?' Peter asked his daughter, suspecting her answer.

'No, Daddy. 'Cos we're not finished. Kyle and Libby need my help,' Sam added importantly.

He surveyed the organized chaos. 'I see they do,' he said wryly.

'We've had fun, which was the main idea,' Libby said.

Peter stared at her. 'You're kind to say that after she's demolished your kitchen.'

'It'll wash.'

Sam tugged on Libby's elbow. 'There's lots of cookies left to decorate. Can my dad help?'

Libby didn't have the heart to wipe the sweet, hopeful expression off Sam's face. She understood how this child had wrapped her father around her every whim. 'If he wants to,' she said, glad for the relaxed atmosphere between them. He obviously hadn't held a grudge since she'd rejected his job offer.

Kyle's and Samantha's eyes shone with excitement. Peter smiled. 'I thought you'd never ask.' Taking off his coat, he disappeared into the living room. A few seconds later he returned, rolling his sleeves over his elbows.

'What shall I do?' he asked, sitting in the chair next to Libby.

Caught up in her notice of his large hands, long, lean fingers and the dark hair dusting his forearms, she couldn't answer. Why did such a typical sight drive coherent thoughts out of her mind? She'd seen his hands, for heaven's sake. *His hands.* What would she do if she ever saw his bare chest?

'Us men can be partners,' Kyle decreed. 'The girls can work together.'

'Sounds fine to me. Have you eaten supper?'

Libby forced her attention away from broad shoulders covered in cotton polyester and a fragrance much more provocative than the scent belonging to the last man who'd sat at her kitchen table—Ralph.

'I'm afraid we ruined our appetites. Everyone sampled too many sweets.' She smeared another star with yellow frosting and handed it to Sam for the colored sugar sprinkles. 'I thought I'd bake a pizza as soon as we finish this batch.'

'I was thinking along the lines of ordering one, but—'

'Yes!' Sam and Kyle screamed together. 'Let's order pizza. Sausage and pepperoni.'

'Is that OK?' he asked her.

Libby mentally reviewed the cash in her billfold. 'I suppose.'

Peter made the phone call, then took his place on the frosting assembly line.

Sam carefully dumped sprinkles on another yellow-frosted star cookie. 'Kyle said we could go with 'em to the Elf's Workshop and see the reindeer.'

'He did?' Peter asked.

Sam nodded. 'And we're going to the Christmas tree farm, too. Right, Libby?'

Libby gulped. She'd invited Sam, but hadn't mentioned Peter. She should have known that 'you' to Samantha meant both Sam *and* her father. 'If your dad wants to come along he's welcome.'

'Plus,' Samantha continued, 'we're going caroling at the nursing home for the old people. They like to hear kids sing. My teacher said so.'

'That's nice.' Peter used an even tone, although again Libby felt his gaze rest on her.

'You'll come with us, won't you, Dr Caldwell?' Kyle sounded worried.

'It's your mother's decision.'

Kyle turned his soulful eyes on Libby. 'He can, can't he?'

In the spotlight of three pairs of eyes, she said the only thing possible. 'Of course.'

'I won't tread on anyone's territory, will I?' he asked. 'A jealous boyfriend or a fiancé?'

If only she could say yes. 'No,' she replied.

Peter smiled. 'Then I'll join you whenever I'm free, but I can't make any promises.'

Sam nudged Kyle. 'That's because he has to take care of sick people.' She glanced over her shoulder toward the counter. 'Are we about done?'

Libby heard the plaintive note in Sam's voice. She, too, was ready to call an end to their endeavors. 'You bet,' she said, scraping green frosting out of the bowl. 'Just a few more.'

As the last cookie had been decorated the doorbell rang. Libby located her purse and began to rummage for her wallet. 'Kyle? You and Sam go to the bathroom and wash your hands. Supper's here.'

The two youngsters scampered to obey, their energy restored. 'I'll pay the delivery boy,' Peter said. 'My treat.'

She opened her mouth to protest, but he shook his head. 'No arguments.' While he strode to the front entrance Libby cleared a spot off the table for their meal. By the time he returned she'd found plates and had started pouring water into plastic tumblers.

'Sam hasn't seen the Charlie Brown Christmas video

yet, Mom,' Kyle announced. 'Can we eat in the living room and watch it?'

'As long as you're careful and don't spill your drinks.'

Carefully balancing their plates and napkins in one hand and their cups in the other, the two youngsters hurried out of the kitchen.

'Active, aren't they?' Peter commented in an off-handed way as he helped himself to several slices of pizza.

Libby carried a stack of dirty bowls to the sink before she sat down with her portion of pepperoni pizza. 'At times I wish I had their energy.'

'Just think what we could accomplish,' he agreed. 'By the way, I don't need a nurse after all.'

'You don't?' She schooled her expression to hide her illogical sense of disappointment.

He shook his head. 'Mavis is staying. Apparently she's convinced her husband to wait another year before they take to the highways.'

'That's nice.' She winced at her inane comment. 'For you, anyway.'

'Yeah, but I almost hate for her to postpone their travel plans. No one knows what tomorrow will bring.'

'Such sage advice,' she said lightly. 'Are you speaking from experience or just philosophizing?'

'A little of both, I guess.'

A speck of tomato sauce clung to the corner of his mouth. She fought the urge to wipe it away, purposely taking a drink to keep her hands busy. She needed more time with adults, she decided. Next thing she knew, she'd reach out and cut his food into little pieces.

Lowering her gaze, she saw a dab of sauce on the button placket of his beige shirt. Having never seen him in anything except an immaculate condition, the flaw made him seem more ordinary, less high-flown. She handed him a napkin. 'I think you need this.'

He glanced down. 'I'm worse than a kid,' he said good-naturedly as he wiped at the spot.

The area grew larger. 'That won't work,' she said, rising. After wetting and wringing out a clean dishcloth, she pivoted and nearly stepped into his arms.

'Thanks,' he said, taking the damp square of fabric from her hand. He rubbed, but the red stain didn't fade.

'Here, let me,' she said, sliding her hand underneath the placket and scrubbing with vehemence. She felt the soft hair on his chest brushing against her knuckles and the warmth emanating from his body.

Libby yanked her hand out as if it were on fire. 'I have a stain remover. Let's try that.' She rushed toward the cabinet where she stored her laundry supplies. By the time she turned around he'd removed his shirt.

She froze. Reality was much better than fantasy. His shoulders were broad and begged to be caressed. His flesh was taut over his ribcage, his muscles firm. She studied the area over his heart, yearning to feel the steady beat beneath her fingertips.

He held out his shirt. 'I thought it would be easier if I took it off.'

Gathering her wits, Libby advanced. 'Won't you be cold?'

'It's warm enough.'

She wiped her forehead with her forearm, certain her rising internal temperature had little to do with the heat generated by the oven. Forcing herself to breathe deeply, she tried to think cool thoughts—Antarctica, penguins, ice—but she wasn't successful.

A few minutes later she'd scrubbed the stain out and towel-dried the wet area, conscious of Peter hovering nearby. 'All done,' she said brightly as she handed him his clothing.

He slid his arms into the sleeves. 'Thanks.'

A coughing sound came from the living room, breaking the spell she'd been under.

'Yours or mine?' Peter joked, buttoning his shirt.

'Must be yours,' Libby returned. 'Kyle hasn't even had a sniffle.'

The harsh sound didn't stop and she exchanged an uneasy glance with him. He pivoted, ready to spring into action as Sam called out in terror. 'Daddy! Come quick!'

Peter dashed out of the kitchen, overturning a chair in the process. Libby followed on his heels.

She gasped at the sight before her. Kyle lay on the floor, his face turning blue while Sam thumped on his back.

'He's choking!' Sam screamed.

Peter moved Sam out of the way, then knelt beside Kyle. 'What happened?'

Sam's face reflected her terror. 'We wasn't horsing around. We was just eating. All of a sudden he started coughing.'

Libby crouched next to her son. 'Can you talk?'

Fear filled Kyle's eyes as he shook his head and struggled for breath.

'Just relax,' she said. 'We'll get it out.'

'Let me.' Without waiting for her approval, Peter picked up Kyle with ease and wrapped his arms around Kyle's waist. Placing the fleshy part of one fist below the child's breastbone and his other hand on top, he pressed upward and inward with a brisk motion.

Nothing happened.

Kyle hung like a rag doll in Peter's arms and Libby

felt the first stirrings of panic. In spite of her training, this was *her* son in trouble.

Peter repeated the Heimlich maneuver. Then again.

Her fear increased with each unsuccessful attempt. She checked the clock, monitoring the time elapsed.

A sheen of sweat appeared on Peter's forehead. 'Come on, Kyle,' he said as he jerked his hands against Kyle's body again.

At that moment a chunk of ground sausage shot across the room like a bullet. Kyle gasped for air, his chest heaving.

Libby's knees wobbled and she sank onto the well-worn sofa. Her fingers trembled as she brushed at fallen wisps of hair, pushing them away from her face.

Peter supported Kyle in his arms. 'How are you doing?'

Kyle nodded, appearing content to remain in Peter's embrace. At long last he wiggled out of Peter's grasp and rubbed a spot on his diaphragm. 'It hurts a little here, but can I have more pizza, Mom?'

Libby softened her sigh with a weak smile. 'I think you need to go back on baby food.'

'Mom!'

'All right. But *chew* before you swallow.'

Kyle turned to Peter, adoration written across his features. 'Thanks, Dr Caldwell.'

Peter ruffled the boy's hair and smiled. 'My pleasure. I think we can dispense with formality, though. Just call me Peter.'

Kyle's head bobbed as a smile spread from ear to ear. 'Great!'

Libby wanted to object, but how could she? The man had saved her son's life.

Oh, my, she thought. For someone who'd never wanted help from a Caldwell, she was certainly glad it had been available. How like Fate to make her eat her words.

'Kids? We'll be in the other room if you need us.' Peter beckoned to Libby. Although she followed, she hated to let Kyle out of her sight.

'Maybe we should sit in here. . .' she said.

Peter frowned and lowered his voice for her ears only. 'He's fine. Hovering over him won't do anything but make him self-conscious.'

She gave Kyle a final glance, then nodded. 'We'll be in the kitchen if you need anything.'

'Sure, Mom.'

'OK.' The two children spoke in unison, without taking their attention off the Charlie Brown television program. They'd obviously dismissed the hair-raising event as unimportant.

In the other room Libby sat at the table and stared at her plate. Her appetite had disappeared and her entire body started to shake.

Peter laid a hand on her shoulder. 'He's fine,' he repeated.

Her mouth quivered. 'I know. I don't understand why I'm reacting like this.'

'I do. He's your son. Your emotional ties are strong. Also, it's been a long day and you're tired.'

His touch felt so good, so comforting, which was surprising in itself. At the moment, however, she didn't see him as the ogre she'd painted him but as the man who'd saved her son.

'You're probably right.'

'I know I am. By the way, the preliminary blood culture reports on Kathy Sanders came this afternoon.'

'And?' she asked, appreciating his diversion tactic.

'Our patient has an *E. coli* septicemia—an infection in her bloodstream. There's good news, though. The drug susceptibility indicates that the antibiotics we're using should be effective.'

'I'm glad. So very glad.' She remembered the days of hovering over Elaine, waiting to win the battle over her pneumonia. Hopefully, Kathy's outcome would be better than Elaine's had been.

'It will be a while before we see any real change, but I'm cautiously optimistic.'

'That's wonderful!'

His gaze became searching. 'You're really involved with this case, aren't you?'

Libby didn't want him asking questions. She shot to her feet and stacked several empty bowls on top of each other.

'I'm involved with all of my patients,' she said, avoiding his eyes.

'I wonder.' He hesitated. 'A young person you knew died, didn't they?'

'Yes.' Turning away, she carried her cargo to the counter.

He followed, apparently waiting for an answer she wasn't willing to give.

Instead, she stoppered the sink, turned on the faucet and squirted dish detergent into the hot water.

'Where's a towel? I'll dry.'

The kitchen was too small for the two of them, or so she thought. 'I can manage.'

'If I'm taking cookies home I'll do my share of the clean-up,' he said in a tone brooking no argument.

She heaved a resigned sigh. 'Top drawer on my right.'

For a few minutes they worked in silence. Finally, Peter raised his voice over the water she'd left running to rinse the dishes. 'Was it renal failure?'

He wouldn't give up until he had the answers he

sought, and she bowed to the inevitable. 'My sister had a form of pneumonia which didn't respond to treatment. Our parents were already gone at that time.' Libby rinsed the suds off another bowl and placed it on the drain rack.

'I'm sorry. Was it recent?'

'About seven years ago.' She purposely neglected to mention they'd moved to Belleville shortly afterward.

After a long silence Peter surprised her with his own story as he dried the dishes.

'My wife and I were invited to a Christmas party one year. She didn't want to wait until my shift ended so we agreed to meet each other at our friend's house.'

Libby slowed her hands in order to make as little noise as possible. Interrupting the tale was out of the question. Curiosity held her captive.

'By the time I arrived several hours later she'd already left. With another man. A colleague, in fact.'

How awful, she thought.

'Unfortunately a drunk driver, courtesy of another Christmas party, sideswiped them. Carol was killed instantly. I learned later that she'd taken her suitcases to the airport earlier in the day. Apparently she'd been planning her getaway for weeks.'

Libby now understood the haunted look in his eyes when she'd first seen him in the elevator. Those intervening years hadn't been easy for him either.

'For a long time I hated Christmas. Everything—the music, the parties, the trees—*everything* reminded me of what Carol had done, how she'd betrayed me. So I didn't celebrate the season. I wiped all traces of the holiday out of the house immediately, even before the funeral had taken place. Sam was four at the time and didn't realize what she was missing.

'A few years ago I tried to get in the spirit, but I

couldn't.' He glanced toward the living room. 'I haven't ever seen Sammie this excited. You've given her an experience that she'll never forget, although I'm a little jealous. I wish I could have done it for her.'

'I remember our first Christmas without my sister,' she said slowly. 'I wanted to forget the holiday, too— pretend it didn't exist. But Christmas is for kids and I knew if I didn't force myself to drag out all the trappings for Kyle's sake it wouldn't be any easier the next time. After we took down the tree and stored the decorations I realized something crucial. The season had become a time of healing, hope and new traditions.'

Peter pinned her with his gaze. 'That's what I want— a healing. I have to relearn the wonders and excitement of Christmas, but before I can experience the holiday with the same hope and joy of a child someone has to show me how to accomplish it. I've forgotten.'

He hesitated. 'I realize you're not overjoyed at having me tag along on your outings—'

Libby studiously examined her bowl while he continued.

'But you have a special rapport with Sam. In my opinion, that makes you the best person—the *only* person—I know who can help me relegate ancient history to where it belongs.' He fell silent. 'If you won't do it for me will you do it for Samantha?'

She wanted to protest. She wanted to give him the name of several people who'd take him under their wing. Yet she couldn't do any of those things.

His request touched her heart in a way she'd never thought possible. In that moment she didn't see a Caldwell but a man plagued by his own Ghost of Christmas Past.

In spite of the repercussions if he ever learned the truth about Kyle, she was still a nurse, dedicated to alleviating human suffering. She couldn't refuse a man who risked rejection in order to be the father his daughter needed.

As for her own dilemma, if Peter hadn't connected her to his cousin's indiscretion by now maybe he never would. Although Kyle would never know of his connection to the Caldwells, at least he'd have one Christmas with a father figure in his life.

'OK,' she said, hoping she wasn't making a major mistake.

'You will? Honestly?'

'Yes.' Heaven help her, but she would.

Peter's face broke into a smile, one she found dazzling and entirely too sexy for her own good.

'I'll do my best to give Samantha a Christmas to remember.'

# CHAPTER FIVE

As THE new week started Christmas plans took on a minor role in Libby's life. Kathy Sanders weighed on her mind and, although she'd hoped to see a miraculous recovery, the young woman's condition remained worrisome. Alarmed by Kathy's lack of response, Libby voiced her concerns to Peter.

'Her urine output hasn't improved,' she stated, showing him the figures. 'It's still low, in spite of her normal blood pressure and fluid intake. Her kidney function results are the same, too.'

Peter flipped through the documents in Kathy's chart. 'I'd hoped to see more positive signs by now, but we can't become discouraged. According to the culture report, we're using the right antibiotic combination. As far as the other tests go, the numbers aren't getting worse.'

'Shouldn't we be doing *something* else?'

'Like what?'

Libby shrugged. 'I don't know. You're the doctor.'

He thrust the file into the designated slot for medical records. 'Continue the IV medication and monitor her fluids. Also watch for signs of cyanosis in her extremities.'

Libby made a mental note to do so. 'May I ask why?'

Peter didn't seem to take offense at her question. 'If she stops producing urine it could mean the fibrin is being deposited in the glomeruli of the kidney, which isn't good. As for her fingers and toes, fibrin deposits in the small vessels could lead to gangrene. If that happens. . .' His voice died.

The prospect was horrifying for someone of any age, much less a young person. 'I'll pay close attention. I'll also stress the importance when I pass along your instructions to the next shift.'

He sat on the countertop and propped one foot on a chair. 'Becky Sanders told me how happy she is about the care Kathy is receiving. She never dreamed her sister would receive so much attention.'

'I'm glad she's satisfied with St Nick's staff.'

'Actually,' he began, 'I think she referred to you.'

Libby's face warmed at the praise. 'I have spent every spare moment I can find with them. Luckily, my other patients aren't as ill so no one's being neglected.'

Peter met her gaze. 'Can you handle the situation if Kathy should take a turn for the worse?'

Libby studied his expression, trying to read between the lines. Her conclusion wasn't encouraging. 'You don't expect her to recover, do you?' she asked in a near-whisper, certain that if she gave full voice to her fears they would come true.

'Like you, I'm hoping for the best. Unfortunately, if it doesn't happen I need a nurse who won't fall apart.'

She squared her shoulders. 'I won't.'

His gaze became intent. 'Maybe I should ask Ann to reassign you.'

'No!' She tempered her tone. 'Just because I lost my sister and know what those two are going through doesn't mean I can't cope.'

'You're sure.'

'Yes.'

He shifted positions, placing both of his black wing-tipped shoes on the floor. 'I'm fairly sure Kathy's outcome will be more favorable. If not, it won't be for lack of trying. I'm following a specialist's advice to the letter.'

'You are?'

'Don't sound so surprised,' he said wryly. 'I don't want to lose a patient any more than you do, especially one with her whole life ahead of her. For your information, I contacted a physician I know—a nephrologist—and faxed copies of Kathy's reports. He's endorsed my treatment protocol.'

She'd never expected him to ask for help or admit he was out of his depth. Obviously, she was wrong. Pondering this new facet to his character, she wondered what other traits she might have unfairly attributed to him.

'Thank you,' Libby said softly.

He stretched to his full height. 'I'd have done the same thing for any other patient. By the way, Sylvia has invited Sam and myself to her house for Thanksgiving dinner tomorrow.'

The holiday suddenly held more appeal. 'Kyle will be thrilled. He's been fretting over the possibility of you two celebrating alone.'

Peter grinned. 'I wasn't sure we could come so I didn't say anything to Sam for fear she'd be disappointed. Silly of me, I suppose, to worry about that.'

'Not really.' She grinned. 'Life has enough misfortunes to deal with—why add to them?' She changed topics, fearing he would grill her for specifics. 'So who's covering your practice?'

'Jerry Moore.'

'Then I'll know who to call if I need a doctor.' At his puzzled expression, she added, 'I'm on duty.'

'Ah-h. So that's why we're not gathering until late afternoon.'

She nodded. 'Sylvia's always planned her dinner

around my schedule, bless her heart. Luckily, she keeps Kyle while I'm working.'

'I hate to arrive empty-handed. What would you suggest I bring?'

'Sylvia makes enough food for the entire block. She doesn't need more.'

'What about a bottle of wine?' he asked.

'Ralph would enjoy a glass, but she won't drink it.' Libby smiled. 'She pretends to be a teetotaler.'

'I'll think of something else.'

'It's OK. Sylvia doesn't really care other than it gives her one more excuse to argue with Ralph.'

'I don't want to cause any friction—'

'You won't,' Libby assured him. 'Friction between those two is a given fact. They thrive on it. Keeps the blood flowing, as Sylvia says.'

'I can think of better ways to get the blood flowing,' he remarked.

So could Libby as she stared at the fabric stretched across Peter's thighs. Liquid heat diffused out from the center of her being.

She glanced at him. From the intent gleam in his eyes and the way he shifted his weight his thoughts had travelled along the same lines.

'Maybe I should pull Ralph aside and give him a few pointers. His disposition might improve.' He winked.

'The man has a cast on an arm and leg. He can't follow your advice—' Peter's raised eyebrow sent her backpedaling. 'Never mind. Forget I said anything.'

'I should say so,' he said. 'People can be quite inventive when the situation warrants. How else do you suppose kids get pregnant in the back seats of cars?'

Reminded of the situation between Elaine and Bryce, she steered the subject off the perilous track. 'Please don't get the wrong idea about Ralph. He really has a marshmallow heart under his gruff exterior.

'During our first winter here we had a terrible snow storm. Ralph shoveled his way to our doorstep, bringing groceries. He was afraid Kyle had run out of milk.' She grinned. 'In spite of his complaining, Ralph has been good to us.'

'For your sakes, I'm glad,' Peter said.

'As for Sylvia, she likes flowers of all kinds. You might consider a plant or a bouquet for your hostess gift.'

'Thanks for the tip.' He turned to leave, then stopped. 'I've told Dr Moore about Ms Sanders, but if you should see a change I'd like to be called.'

'I will,' Libby promised.

Over the next few hours she diligently carried out Peter's latest instructions. Although Kathy's condition remained the same, Libby refused to lose hope. During each trip into Kathy's room she mentally willed her patient to recover.

After punching the time clock, she arrived at the school to bring Kyle and Samantha home. Expecting to see Kyle race to the car as he usually did, she was surprised to watch him trudge to the car and slide in beside her.

'I don't feel so good, Mom,' he whined. 'My throat hurts.'

Libby reached over and felt his forehead. A pale face, warm skin, and dull eyes told their own story.

Samantha scampered into the rear seat of Libby's Dodge Colt station wagon. 'Is he gonna miss Thanksgiving dinner?'

'I don't know, Sammie,' she replied, conscious of using Peter's pet name. 'We'll have to wait and see.'

She left Sam in Mrs Bridges's care, before hurrying to their own house. Once inside, she helped Kyle remove his coat, then popped a thermometer in his mouth.

One hundred two degrees Fahrenheit. She sighed. 'Open wide so I can take a look at your tonsils.'

Kyle obeyed. The patchy bright red throat was a familiar sight. His previous bouts with strep throat had taught her to diagnose his infection without cultures and blood tests.

He stared at her, fear on his face. 'Is it—?'

She flung her arms around his shoulders. 'Afraid so, sport.'

'I don't want a shot.' His lower lip quivered before a mulish set came to his face.

'You may not have a choice,' she said, trying to prepare him for the inevitable. 'I'll call the doctor and see what he wants to do.' She hugged him, before going to the phone and dialing the number from memory.

'I'm sorry,' the receptionist stated as soon as Libby explained Kyle's situation. 'Dr Downey hasn't returned from his cruise and Dr Moore's busy with a delivery. Dr Caldwell could see him, though.'

'He probably wouldn't consider phoning a prescription to the pharmacy, would he?' Libby asked, suspecting that the answer would be no but feeling she had to try.

'Since he's never seen Kyle before, I'm sure he won't,' the woman said. 'If you'll wait on the line, though, I'll ask—'

'Never mind,' she said wearily, contemplating the cost when her medical account still showed an unpaid balance. Yet what choice did she have? Home remedies weren't effective against this infection, and the risks of complications such as rheumatic fever were too great to contemplate.

'We've had a four-o'clock cancellation so if you could bring him in—'

'We're on our way.'

After a quick trip across town Libby was pleasantly surprised to be ushered into an exam room minutes after they'd arrived.

Peter strode in, his white coat flapping about his knees and a stethoscope peeking out of a pocket. 'Feeling poorly, son?'

His form of address was generic and yet Libby couldn't help but notice how Kyle's eyes had seemed to perk up.

Kyle nodded. 'My throat hurts,' he whispered. 'Mom says it's strep.'

'She does? Mind if I take a look for myself?'

Kyle opened his mouth wide and Peter peered inside. A few seconds later he straightened.

'You have a smart mother,' Peter said, checking Kyle's ears. 'That's my diagnosis, too. Ordinarily, I'd run a throat culture to confirm it—'

'It's not necessary,' Libby interrupted, hoping to dissuade him. Even without the test, the cost of Kyle's illness would strain her tight budget. She fingered the frayed edge of her coat, wondering where she could cut a few more financial corners.

'But we can get by without one,' he finished.

She glanced at him in relief. Seeing how his attention lingered on her nervous actions, she thrust her fists into her coat pockets.

Peter laid a hand on Kyle's shoulder. 'The best and fastest way to get rid of this infection is a shot.'

Kyle's chin quivered and he sent a pleading look toward Libby before he stared up at Peter. 'You can't give me any pills?'

'They'd be tough to swallow, don't you think?'

'Mom could grind them up,' Kyle said helpfully.

Peter crossed one arm over his chest and rested his elbow on his hand. With two fingers wrapped around his chin and an index finger along his jawline, he appeared to give Kyle's suggestion some thought. 'Yes, but if we go that route you might not be well enough to help Sam and me cut down our Christmas tree this weekend.'

Kyle wrinkled his face in thought. 'Sam would be disappointed. I said I'd teach her what to look for.'

'You could tell her, I suppose, but it wouldn't be the same as if you were there,' Peter said.

Kyle drew a deep breath. His shoulders straightened. 'OK. A shot.'

Libby hid her smile. Peter's tactics had produced the desired effect without engaging in battle.

'But it better not hurt,' Kyle added.

'It will for just a short time, but I know you're tough enough to handle it,' Peter said. He flipped through Kyle's records. 'The injection will be a long-acting form of penicillin. Are either of you allergic to any medication?'

Libby answered. 'No.'

Peter scribbled a note on the clipboard. 'Any more nose-bleeds?'

Libby's 'no' and Kyle's 'yes' came simultaneously.

'I had one the other day at school,' Kyle said, 'but it wasn't bad. I didn't even have to go to the nurse's office.'

'You should have said something,' Libby chided.

'It was no big deal, Mom. I can take care of myself.'

Libby exchanged an amused glance with Peter. He tucked the clipboard under one arm, strode to the door and opened it. 'Mavis will be in shortly. Once you're home stay in bed and rest. No friends for at least twenty-four hours until your fever is gone.'

'But. . .but tomorrow is Thanksgiving,' Kyle protested.

Peter paused. He closed the door. 'That is a problem, isn't it?'

Kyle nodded. Libby had her own concerns to sort through. She couldn't call in sick as the hospital staffed the holidays with minimal coverage. Yet she couldn't send Kyle to Sylvia's as she'd planned. Exposing Ralph, Sylvia and Samantha to strep wasn't the sensible thing to do.

'You're working tomorrow, right?' he asked Libby.

'Yes, but they'll have to find someone else. I can't leave Kyle home alone.' Although she'd volunteered to work the holiday for the benefit of the additional pay, she'd find another means to earn enough money for Kyle's Christmas bicycle.

'Did Sylvia intend to keep Kyle all day?'

Libby nodded.

He shrugged one shoulder. 'Then the solution's obvious. We'll switch kids. Sam can go to her house and Kyle and I will spend the day watching the parades and football games on television. After you come home we'll go to Sylvia's, provided Kyle's temperature is co-operating.'

Kyle's dull eyes flashed. 'That's a great idea!'

A portion of Libby saw how Peter's suggestion was perfect, but her old habit of worrying about contact between her son and the Caldwells reared its head. She'd resigned herself to allowing Peter and his daughter into their lives, but she'd always imagined that *she* would be there to keep tabs on the conversation. Her agreement didn't include Kyle and Peter being alone.

Still, she couldn't bypass a tailor-made solution. Kyle would love spending the day with a man he so clearly idolized and, besides, she needed the paycheck.

'Are you sure you don't want quality time with Sam tomorrow?'

Peter's grin became lopsided. 'She's more interested in learning how to bake a turkey with all the trimmings.'

'Then I accept your offer.'

'All right!' Kyle's exuberance was weak and his smile wan—all indications of how poorly he felt—but it was obvious that he considered the new plan as a more attractive alternative to being Sylvia's assistant.

'I'll see you both early in the morning. Bye.'

Libby mentally reviewed her pantry. She hadn't planned to prepare lunch at all and now she had to arrive at a meal appropriate for a sick little boy and a healthy adult male.

Chicken noddle soup, she decided. And gelatin. If Peter didn't care for the light diet he could console himself with Sylvia's feast later in the day.

To Libby's surprise, Peter returned brandishing two glass syringes. Kyle's eyes widened in fear. 'Are those *both* for me?'

'One's for you. The other's for your mom.'

Alarm skidded down Libby's spine. Knowing that the injection was usually administered in the gluteal muscle, the thought of baring her hip—even modestly—to this man who reeked of virility was enough to send her into cardiac arrest.

The only good thing about the situation was that, thanks to not finishing her laundry chores last night, she'd worn her only pair of satin undies. For some strange reason, and to her dismay, a feminine ache stirred in her body.

She crossed her legs. 'Where's Mavis?' she asked, hoping she didn't sound as nervous as she felt.

'Busy. I'm her stand-in. But don't worry, I'm as good

as she is.' His grin revealed straight, pearly white teeth.

Peter gave Kyle the pediatric-dosage injection while Libby sat in strained silence.

'You did great,' Peter said, dropping the used syringe into the sharps container. 'Mom's turn.'

'No pills?' she asked, keeping her tone light.

'And risk missing the opportunity to join us in the great Christmas tree search?'

'It doesn't hurt,' Kyle encouraged. 'Dr Caldwell does it fast so it'll be over before you know it.'

Libby slid off her coat and rolled up her right shirt sleeve.

Peter cleared his throat. 'Not much muscle on you, is there? I'd rather use another site.'

She was ready to refuse until she saw Kyle follow the proceedings with interest. Further balking on her part would draw even more attention. 'Oh, all right,' she muttered.

'If you'd rather administer it yourself. . .' His voice raised was in question as he held out the syringe.

Libby tugged her shirt out of her uniform trousers. 'Go ahead.'

He walked behind her as she lowered the waistband a few inches and presented her hip to him. Conscious of his proximity, feeling the heat emanating from him and smelling his special brand of cologne, she jumped as he applied the cool antiseptic.

'I haven't done anything yet,' he said in her ear, clearly amused.

Kyle giggled.

Libby tensed, aware of Peter's warm fingers on her bare skin.

'Just relax,' Peter crooned.

If only she could. If he were sixty-year-old Dr Downey, instead of a handsome young doctor, she'd do so without any qualms. But he wasn't, and she couldn't.

The sting came and went. 'That's it,' Peter said, dropping the used equipment in the disposal unit. 'See you both tomorrow.' With that, he strode from the room.

'Well, Mom?' Kyle asked. 'It wasn't so bad, was it?'

'No, it wasn't,' she agreed, knowing he referred to the procedure itself. At the same time she berated herself for overreacting. Peter had administered the shot in the same professional manner he would have used on an eighty-year-old woman. He was totally unaffected and she was being ridiculous to think otherwise.

She quickly rearranged her clothes and tugged on her well-worn coat, anxious to put this experience behind her. 'Let's go home.'

Peter strode from the room, anxious to physically distance himself from Libby. He'd never imagined that the three inches of skin he'd seen would be so alluring. Of course, the white silk she wore under her uniform hadn't helped. Neither had the light floral fragrance or the clean scent in her hair.

Thank goodness she was Downey's patient. He'd be hard pressed to maintain his professional attitude if he saw her in a state of total undress. He grinned at the appealing thought.

How ironic to be attracted to a woman who didn't seem to delight in his attention. And yet, he wondered... Her obvious disquiet in his exam room wasn't the usual reaction he encountered, especially from someone who'd given birth and was also a nurse. Perhaps Ms Brown wasn't as immune to him as she acted.

The following days would prove interesting. He intended to discover if her hands-off attitude was genuine or merely a ploy fueled by bad experiences. For the first time since his wife had left him excitement over the coming holidays stirred in his chest, and he knew it was all because of Libby.

The following afternoon Libby approached her house, surprised to find the curtains still drawn. Quiet greeted her as she stepped inside. Feeling like Goldilocks, she checked each room to find it empty. Her own bedroom, however, presented a different sight.

She paused in the doorway, noticing the two figures in stockinged feet sprawled across her pink floral comforter. Two heads lay close together—a picture of familial tranquility. An open picture-book about dinosaurs lay over Peter's flat stomach.

Leaning against the frame, Libby smiled. Kyle loved to rest in her bed whenever he was ill. Obviously he'd convinced Peter to read him a story and the two had fallen asleep.

She studied her son's face and found the tell-tale flush of fever remaining on his cheeks. Without feeling his forehead or relying on a temperature reading, she knew he wouldn't be well enough to celebrate at Sylvia's house tonight.

Her attention drifted to the man beside him. The lines and planes of Peter's face were darkened with five-o'clock shadow even though it was shortly past three. After hearing about a difficult delivery in the wee hours of the morning, which had resulted in mother and baby being airlifted to a tertiary care facility, she understood how he'd succumbed to the peaceful afternoon.

Having crawled out of bed every few hours to bathe Kyle's forehead with a cool cloth to settle his restless movements, she'd have taken a nap, too.

Kyle rolled over and the book draped over Peter

thudded onto the floor. Peter stirred and Libby felt like a voyeur as she watched him awaken. Yet the experience was so electrifying, so arousing, so heart-warming, that she couldn't force herself to leave.

Peter glanced at her. His eyes widened in recognition and she waggled her fingers in hello. He cautiously levered himself off the bed without disturbing Kyle—an art perfected by parenthood.

He followed her into the kitchen. 'Sorry you caught me dozing,' he said, rubbing his face. 'I must have been more tired than I thought.'

The rasp of his whiskers was decidedly provocative. 'Napping is one of my favorite pastimes, too, so don't worry about it.' She grinned. 'I won't fire you for sleeping on the job.'

He pulled out a chair. 'What a relief!'

'How's Kyle?'

'Puny. He didn't eat much, although I think he went through an entire box of popsicles, nearly all of the gelatin and most of your fruit juice. By the way, I thought the soup was delicious.'

Her face warmed. 'Thanks.'

'His temp is coming down but it isn't normal yet.'

'I didn't expect it to be. I'm afraid we won't be sharing dinner with you.'

'I'll bring you a doggie bag,' Peter promised.

Libby rested her elbows on the table. 'Then you two managed without any problems?'

He leaned back in his chair. 'Absolutely. Kyle's a great kid. You should be proud of him.'

'I am.'

'He's really excited about finding the right Christmas trees for both of us. I'm afraid we'll spend the entire day at the tree farm, traipsing over miles of ground in search of the perfect pine.'

'Probably,' she agreed. 'Be sure to dress warmly when we go.'

His watch beeped. 'I suppose I should head for home and shower before dinner.' He rubbed his face again. 'Can't go looking like a bum.'

Libby was certain that if all derelicts looked as good as he did in his jeans and sweatshirt, emblazoned with the University of Kansas jayhawk, there wouldn't be any homeless people. Her fingers itched to run along the soft fleece and trace his comforting shoulders, his muscular biceps, his rock-hard ribcage.

She swallowed hard.

'By the way, how was work?' he asked.

'Work?' Her mind drew a blank before she refocused her thoughts. 'It was rather slow, which was nice for a change. Kathy Sanders looked much better and definitely more alert. She even asked to wash her hair.'

'A sure sign of recovery in a woman,' he joked.

'And how do you gauge if a *man* is feeling better?'

'It's simple. He complains about the food.' He winked.

She laughed. 'You're probably right. In any event, Kathy's lab results showed an improvement as well. The fibrinogen level is higher than on her last report and so is her platelet count.'

'I know. I called the lab this morning.'

'You did?'

Peter's mouth twisted into a sheepish-looking grin. 'Couldn't stand the suspense.' He glanced at his watch. 'I'd better run if I'm supposed to get Ralph and be next door by five-thirty.'

Oddly enough, she wanted him to stay. 'Then don't be late,' she said, her tone overly bright. 'Sylvia's a stickler for a time schedule.'

While he slipped on his jogging shoes and tied

the laces, she located his jacket. 'Thanks for watching Kyle.'

'My pleasure.' He wrapped the wool scarf around his throat, before zipping his parka.

She accompanied him to the front door. 'Be careful. It's snowing a little.'

'I will.' He turned on the threshold to face her. 'I'm sorry you can't join us this evening. To be honest, I was looking forward to sharing the occasion with you and Kyle.'

Shocked by his admission, she couldn't speak. His dark gaze, however, locked onto hers. The intensity she saw told her that the attraction she felt was mutual.

Her voice came out barely above a whisper. 'Me too.'

Her heartfelt reply brought a smile to his face. Standing close enough to count the freckles across her nose, he said, 'Once he's better we'll make up for lost time.'

'Think so?'

He nodded. 'Keep Sunday free.'

'Afternoon or evening?'

His eyes gleamed. 'I want the whole day.'

# CHAPTER SIX

BY SUNDAY Kyle was back to his old self. Although he chafed at his enforced inactivity, the anticipation of embarking on the Christmas tree search kept his spirits high.

'Wouldn't it be great if we could do this every year?' he asked, hopping around as he tugged on his snow boots.

Libby smiled at his enthusiasm. 'We do.'

'Naw, I mean take Sam and her dad with us.'

'Let's concentrate on this Christmas before we anticipate the next one,' she said firmly, not wanting to tempt fate by planning too far into the future. 'A lot can happen between now and then.'

She dug two old parkas out of the back of the closet— one large, one small—conscious of the rips she'd handstitched to hold the stuffing and prolong the garments' usefulness. Having served their purpose well over the years, both should have been retired long ago. Yet she kept them for occasions such as this. No sense in ruining their good coats with tree sap or sharp pine needles.

'Maybe someday we could share a big tree with Sam instead of each getting our own.'

Libby handed him a pair of gloves. His innocent tone seemed too innocent, his hopeful expression too hopeful. While she and Kyle might associate with Peter and Samantha, anything more than neighborly friendliness was out of the question and utterly forbidden.

'If you don't want a tree this year,' she said, feigning

bewilderment in spite of his blatant hint, 'we'll only get one for—'

'Sharing means being in the same house together. The four of us.' His usually bright eyes sparkled more. 'Then we could hang our stockings on a *real* fireplace. Sam says we'd have to get one for her dad, though. It wouldn't be fair if the three of us had one and he didn't.'

The scarf she'd wrapped around her throat suddenly seemed too tight, the parka too warm. 'So you've discussed this with Samantha?'

'Sure, Mom. We have it all figured out.' He flipped his hand-knitted muffler around his neck, zipped his coat and pulled the flaps of a battered cap over his head and ears.

Libby purposely kept her tone light. 'What exactly do you have figured out?'

'We'd get married. Wouldn't that be a good idea?'

Perhaps if any other man besides Peter Caldwell were involved. . . Unfortunately, Kyle's suggestion was out of the question. To make matters worse, she couldn't explain her reasons to Kyle. Her mind raced with excuses until she found one she thought acceptable.

'It might, but we're just friends,' she said, trying to forget the unseemly tingling sensation she always felt while in Peter's presence.

'Married people start out as friends. You told me love grows when grown-ups spend time together.'

Kyle had obviously learned a previous lesson well and was now turning her sage advice against her. 'Sometimes that happens. But not always.' The doorbell rang, giving her a grateful reprieve.

'They're here!' Kyle's boots thumped on the floor as he hurried to welcome their visitors.

Peter and Samantha stood on the porch, also dressed

in thick clothing to meet the elements. 'Everybody ready?' Peter asked.

'You bet!' Kyle brushed past him to join Sam.

Libby pulled on a pair of work gloves. 'I'll lead the way, if you'd like.'

'Not necessary,' Peter said. 'Since a tree won't fit in my Honda Eldon loaned me his truck. We can ride together.'

'Great.' After pocketing her house keys and grabbing a sack containing a Thermos of cinnamon-flavored apple cider and four cups, Libby hurried after him.

At the sight of a late-model black Chevrolet truck parked on the driveway, she stopped short. The chrome sparkled and the paint gleamed as if it had been recently washed and waxed.

'Nice, isn't it?' Peter asked, his awe evident.

She started to walk down the steps. 'It's beautiful.'

Peter grabbed her sleeve. 'Watch the ice.'

Looking at her feet, Libby saw the tell-tale sheen on the concrete. 'Thanks,' she said, breathless from the feel of his fingers clasped around her arm rather than from the cold air.

At the base of the stairs he released his hold. 'All aboard!' he said, sliding into the driver's seat.

Kyle and Sam broke apart from their huddle by the rear fender and scampered to the passenger side ahead of Libby. 'Can I sit by the door?' Kyle asked, his breath fogging the air.

Libby eyed the interior. It was spacious, but with four bodies—even though two were small—the quarters would be tight. 'Better not,' she answered. Although the idea of sitting next to Peter quickened her pulse, maintaining a careful distance seemed more sensible. 'I don't want you to fall out.'

Kyle rolled his eyes. 'I'll have my seat belt on.'

'The locks engage as soon as the engine's in gear,' Peter said. 'He can pull the handle all he wants but the door won't open.'

With her excuse eliminated, Libby yielded. 'OK.'

'And I want to sit by Kyle,' Samantha declared, her face set with determination.

That left only one place for Libby—next to Peter. She glanced at Kyle, then Samantha. Their angelic expressions spoke of an obvious attempt to create the blended family they wished to have. Vowing to speak with Kyle later about his matchmaking, she managed a weak smile. 'Well, then. Shall we go?'

She climbed in and slid next to the steering-wheel. Placing the tall Thermos at her feet, she left a respectful distance between Peter and herself. But even with Sam's little body snuggled up against hers, Kyle protested his lack of space. 'Move over, Mom. I can't get in.'

By the time everyone was in and seat belts fastened, Libby found herself plastered against Peter. Even though he wore a leather jacket and she a bulky coat, she was conscious of his triceps resting against her breast and his hip and his long, lean thigh touching hers.

She felt totally unclothed.

Her wiggles to add distance did nothing more than send the inner heat pulsing through her veins at a faster pace. She stopped moving. 'Sorry,' she murmured.

'It is rather snug,' he agreed. His breath skittered across her cheek and he grinned. 'But I'm not complaining.'

Warmth rose in her face. 'Do you need directions?'

His eyes held a wicked gleam, as if he'd placed a risqué connotation on her question.

'To the Holley tree farm,' she clarified. Mortification swept over her.

Peter's lopsided smile appeared. He started the engine

and backed into the street. 'Ah, yes. The tree farm. Eldon said to get on US Highway 283 and drive for about thirty minutes.'

'It's on the left side of the road,' she said.

'Do most people in town have a name associated with Christmas?' he asked, stretching his arm along the back of the seat and resting his palm against Libby's opposite shoulder.

Libby nearly forgot to breathe.

'We don't,' Kyle piped in.

'Neither do we,' Samantha echoed.

'Maybe we should change our name to "Greene" instead of "Brown",' Kyle added helpfully.

'What could we change ours to?' Sam asked, clearly not wanting to be left out.

'Caldwell. Cald well.' Judging from Kyle's tone and his screwed-up face, he was considering the matter seriously. His expression brightened. 'Sleigh bell rhymes with Cald well. You could be Samantha Sleigh Bell.'

Sam giggled. Libby grinned. Peter laughed. Pressed against his side, she felt the rumble coming from his chest. His chuckle sounded rusty at first, as if he hadn't expressed himself so wholeheartedly in a long time. Then it grew deeper. Contentment stole over her like a downy blanket.

'That's silly,' Sam said. 'Let's think of something else.'

While the two continued their nonsense Libby said to Peter, 'According to local history, the early settlers couldn't decide on a name for their community because they didn't want to single out any family.

'In any case, the locals asked for suggestions and some bright child mentioned "Belleville" because it reminded him of Christmas. No one made the connection until he pointed out certain members of the community. The Holleys, Kings, Klauses, Winters, and Shepards lived here.'

'Obviously their descendants haven't moved.'

Libby smiled. 'No.'

He switched lanes of traffic to merge onto the highway. 'I have a favor to ask,' he said in a low voice. She had to strain her ears to hear over the engine. 'But don't feel obligated to say yes. It's rather presumptuous of me to bring the subject up at this late date, but. . .'

'What is it?'

'Whatever tree we choose, Sam really wants you to help us decorate it. She's convinced it won't be special unless we have your input. If you don't have time, though, just say so. I'll make some excuse.'

'What do *you* want?'

'I'd appreciate the help. I want to make up for what she's missed in the past and, to be honest,' he said with a grin, 'I'm artistically challenged.'

'But your home is beautiful,' she protested, thinking of his living room decor.

'Thanks to an interior designer. So will you. . .?'

His desperation and plea touched her heart. How could she turn down making a child's Christmas special? 'I'd be honored.'

He glanced at her, before turning his attention back onto the traffic. 'You're sure?'

'I wouldn't have agreed otherwise.'

'Look, Mom!' Kyle pointed ahead. 'We're here.'

'How time flies,' Peter murmured. Libby silently concurred, wishing the drive had taken longer. She consoled herself by anticipating the trip home.

After parking in the graveled area, they sauntered inside the metal building filled with people who also intended to find their Christmas trees.

Garlands of holly were draped across doorways,

shelves, mantelpieces and a mock bannister. Libby pictured the spindles of Peter's staircase draped with the greenery and accented with red velvet bows. For a brief moment she allowed herself to be envious, then banished the thought. No sense in wishing for the impossible.

Meandering through the small crowd, she watched Samantha's eyes grow wide as she observed trees of all shapes and sizes decorated for the season.

Sam stopped in front of a three-foot pine completely covered with Disney figures. 'Oh, Daddy. Look at this one.'

Peter came to her side. 'Is this what you want?'

Sam glanced at Libby, as if wanting her approval.

'Cartoon characters make a pretty tree,' Libby said, guessing the astronomical cost of the ornaments, 'but why don't we look around before you decide? Kyle and I always have a hard time choosing so we make our own.'

Sam tipped her head upward to stare at Libby with wide eyes. 'Really?' she asked.

'Oh, yes. We string popcorn, cut out snowflakes and stars and create lots of different things. But first,' Libby said, 'we have to find the perfect tree.'

She guided Samantha past the displays to the door leading outside. Wendell Holley, a middle-aged man in blue-striped overalls, handed Peter a map of the property and a hacksaw.

'Nice-looking family,' he said in a loud voice. 'You folks been here before?'

'Yes,' Libby said. 'But—'

Before she could correct his erroneous assumption he interrupted. 'Then you know the layout. This year the trees in section B and C are ready.' He pointed to the sheet. 'Be sure to stay away from the lake. It isn't frozen clear through yet. I've roped it off but kids don't always pay attention. Have a nice time.' Having delivered his admonition, he turned to greet another customer.

They strode into the early afternoon sunshine. After a quick conference around the bonfire they decided to visit section C first. Ambling off together, it struck Libby as a picture of domesticity. It wasn't difficult to pretend they were a family—she'd never planned on spending her life alone. Although she had Kyle, underneath she wished for the same things Kyle did.

Chattering like magpies, Kyle and Sam rushed ahead. 'Don't go too far,' Libby called out. 'Stay where we can see you.'

'We will,' the two chorused.

Peter inhaled deeply. 'Smells good out here.'

'Doesn't it?'

A shout caught her attention. Two figures in the distance were jumping up and down and waving. 'Kyle and Sam must have found something,' she said.

'I never thought it would be this easy,' he said. 'I envisioned spending hours here.'

'Don't worry, we will. Whenever Kyle's seen the so-called perfect tree, one in the distance will catch his eye.'

The two strode ahead, following the trail of small footprints in the snow. A few minutes later they had surrounded a four-foot pine.

'Is this the one you want?' Libby asked, noticing how pine needles fell from it easily, as if it were dying.

Kyle studied the tree from all angles. 'Maybe not. We'll keep looking.' He and Sam took off.

Libby shared a wry smile with Peter.

For the next hour they tramped through rows of trees, studiously examining each one before outlining its merits and faults. Finally, Kyle made his selection.

'Leave a few of the bottom branches,' he said importantly as Peter knelt on the ground to saw the trunk. 'That way, a new tree will grow in its place.'

'I see,' Peter said, moving the blade to the spot Kyle indicated. Before long the pine tumbled over.

'Now what?' Peter asked, dusting the snow off his pants legs.

Libby grabbed hold of the freshly cut end. 'We haul it back to our truck. Unless you want to drag it around with us.'

Peter nudged her aside and started pulling the tree behind him. 'Not a chance. Come on, troops. Fall in.'

After Mr Holley had measured the pine and Peter had hoisted it into the truck bed the search continued in section B. The two children ran ahead, their voices carrying over the white-blanketed countryside.

'I hope Sam makes up her mind soon,' Peter said, holding out his hand to help Libby around tree stumps.

'Don't tell me you're tired?'

He grinned. 'OK, I won't.' He pointed to the Thermos she now carried. 'When can we stop for a break?'

Libby pointed to a bench fashioned out of fallen logs. It stood a short distance away under a row of walnut trees lining the edge of the Holley property. 'As soon as we get there.'

They tramped to their destination, the snow crunching beneath their feet. Before long the four of them were enjoying their cups of hot cider.

Peter stretched out his long legs and leaned back. 'Mmm,' he said. 'This hits the spot.'

'You make the bestest cider,' Sam said, a reddish mustache appearing on her upper lip.

'Have you found the tree you want?' Libby asked the little girl.

Sam wrinkled her face. 'There's an awful lot to pick from,' she said. 'Daddy? What happens with the trees that no one takes home?'

'They grow another year, I suppose,' he answered.

'But what if they're all crooked and their branches aren't pretty?'

Peter shrugged and glanced at Libby, clearly at a loss. 'Mr Holley probably leaves some to be homes for the birds and chops down others to make room for new trees. Why?'

Sam jumped up and handed her cup to Libby. 'I think I found the one I want.'

Peter raised his styrofoam cup. 'As soon as I finish this we'll cut it down.'

'OK. Come on, Kyle, let's go.'

'Stay where we can see you,' Libby reminded them. A gust of wind rattled the branches overhead and a few flakes of snow drifted down. She shivered.

'Cold?' he asked.

'A little.'

Peter patted the log next to him. 'This seat's not taken.'

Her discomfort overruled her logic and she slid across beside him. He flung one arm around her, drawing her close. 'Better?' he asked.

Her breath caught in her throat. She nodded.

'By the way,' he began, 'I never told you about Sylvia and Ralph. They didn't argue once the night we were there.'

Libby stared at him. 'You're kidding.'

He crossed his legs at the ankles. 'I'm not. Ask Sylvia yourself. Of course it might have helped that I brought a bottle of white wine for Ralph and a poinsettia for Sylvia.'

'How diplomatic.'

She glanced at the children in the distance. 'I can't believe they didn't bicker. That's so out of character. I wonder if Ralph was ill.'

'Lovesick is my diagnosis.'

'Come, now—' she began.

'Honest. Sylvia never moved without touching Ralph in some way,' he continued. 'Whether it was passing the food, pouring the coffee—whatever—he didn't seem to mind. In fact, I'd say he enjoyed it.'

She met his gaze. 'Really?'

He nodded. 'I went into the kitchen at one point and nearly caught them stealing a kiss.'

Had the sparks of discord she'd seen for years become sparks of another sort? It seemed totally inconceivable. Still. . .'You're not joking, are you?'

'Nope. I wouldn't joke about something so important.' He placed his palm against the side of her face and hesitated, as if wanting a sign of either encouragement or rejection.

She swallowed. Holding her position, she focused on his full lips hovering a breath away.

He cupped her chin, lowering his mouth slowly and purposely.

As if he were a piece of forbidden fruit, she craved a sample. Unfulfilled desires prevailed over inhibitions. Eager, she leaned forward.

His mouth pressed against hers; his kiss electrified her entire body. He pulled her to his chest and she didn't resist.

She felt his warmth, tasted the cinnamon and apple in his mouth and delighted in the masculine fragrance surrounding him. The pervading aroma of pine and the crisp air enhanced her senses. From now on she'd always associate the outdoor essence with this heady occasion.

If only it were spring, or summer, she thought inanely. Not winter. If only this encounter could take place when thick clothing wasn't in the way.

She stroked his back, remembering the sleek muscles and hard sinews she'd seen. How fortunate she'd removed her gloves earlier.

Her fingers trailed upward. Tracing his cheek-bones and the hollows of his clean-shaven cheeks, she noticed the differences in texture between his skin and hers.

The wind whistled through the bare branches again and snow drifted down. Cold flakes landed on her nose, startling her out of her sensual lethargy.

He straightened. 'Still cold?'

'No.' Her voice came out low and sultry.

His satisfied smile made her heart swell in her chest. 'Good. Then we did it right.'

'I'd say so,' she said, leaning against him.

Frantic calls broke through Libby's contentment. She straightened, searching unsuccessfully for Kyle and Sam. Realizing they weren't in sight, she jumped to her feet while she scanned the horizon. 'Oh, my gosh! Where are the kids?'

At that moment Kyle ran toward them, his familiar blue coat a blur. Sam trailed behind, her legs pumping as fast as she could.

'Mom! Peter! Come quick! Someone's fallen in the lake!'

Libby took off, not surprised that Peter's long legs covered the distance much faster than hers. He grabbed Kyle's arm. 'Where?'

Kyle pointed in a northerly direction. 'Just beyond those trees.'

Libby followed Peter as they hurried through the rows of trees, ignoring the evergreen branches stabbing at them with ferocity. A few minutes later they had passed through the natural obstacle course and found the farm pond Mr Holley had warned them to avoid.

A young boy lay on the ice near the middle of the lake, hanging onto a half-submerged dog trying to find its footing. An occasional sob shook his frame.

'Oh, dear God.' Libby sent a silent prayer upward. The child couldn't have been much older than Kyle and her mother's heart jumped into her throat.

'Hang on, son,' Peter called out. 'I'm coming.'

'You can't,' the boy screamed. 'The ice is breaking.'

'Crawl backward to me.'

'My puppy fell in. He can't get out by himself. I can't leave him.'

Peter turned to Kyle. 'Run to the office. Tell Mr Holley to call 911.'

Kyle disappeared. Peter pointed to the rope cordoning off the area. 'I need something to tie around me.'

Libby hurried to the fence on the right side. The cord was frozen hard and the knot uncooperative, but she pressed on. In the background she heard Peter encouraging the child. Finally the knot loosened and she rushed toward Peter with the freed end.

He looped the thick rope around his waist. 'Leave it attached,' he said, his eyes intent.

She nodded. If the ice broke rescuers could pull him out of the frigid water. 'Be careful.'

Peter inched forward on hands and knees to spread his weight over a larger area. The distance between him and the boy narrowed.

'Don't come any closer,' the boy sobbed. 'I hear the ice cracking!'

Peter returned to solid ground, his expression grim. 'I hate to say it, but even if he let go of the dog I doubt he could crawl back on his own.'

'Let me try,' Libby said. He appeared skeptical, but

she pointed out the obvious. 'We can't wait here and do nothing. Who knows who long it will be until more help arrives?'

He undid the knot and refastened the rope around her waist. 'Don't go out any farther than you have to. And go slowly.'

'I will.'

'Get a good hold on him. I'll pull both of you.'

'OK.' Libby belly-crawled onto the frozen pond.

'Easy,' Peter called.

She slowed. 'What's your name?' she asked the boy. From her position a few arm's lengths away she heard his teeth chattering.

'Bil-Bil-Billy.'

'Where do you live, Billy?'

'N-next farm. . .'

'How's your dog?'

'He's. . .awful. . .cold.'

'Don't worry,' she said, testing each section before easing her way forward. 'We'll have you both home and warm before you know it.'

A distinct crack rent the air and she saw water lap over a new seam only a few feet to her left. Time was running out.

Libby moved again, aware of their precarious position. A few seconds later she grabbed one of Billy's feet. 'If I hold your legs can you hang onto your dog?'

'I. . .I think so.'

'Then here we go.' She gripped his boots near the ankles and called over her shoulder. 'We're ready.'

The rope tightened around her waist and she felt herself being pulled back. In just those few minutes her hands had become numb. She could imagine how the boy's must feel after being exposed to near-freezing water as well.

Dragged inch by inch, a chill seeped through her coat and jeans along the entire length of her body. Her teeth began to chatter. Staring ahead, she saw more and more of Billy's arms until, at long last, a motionless, sodden mass appeared. From the size of it she guessed it was a golden retriever.

Relief flooded through her. They would make it.

On the heels of that realization, she discovered a new problem.

'Stop!' she screamed. The rope grew slack.

'What's wrong?' Peter called.

'I'm pulling his boots off. Wait a minute.' She inched forward, this time wrapping her numb fingers around the calves of Billy's legs. 'How're you doing, Billy?'

'Cold. So cold,' he mumbled.

She hoped his hypothermia was mild. 'Go ahead, Peter. And hurry.'

Once again the rope tightened. Soon the ice beneath her felt more secure and she released her hold. 'Stop,' she called out. By the time she'd sat up and crawled to Billy's side, Peter was already there. In the distance she heard voices and a far-off siren.

'It's OK, sport,' Peter told him, placing the animal in Libby's outstretched arms. 'We'll take care of your dog.'

'His name's Ranger.'

'I'll tell the vet,' Libby said, watching Peter scoop the boy into his arms and hurry off the ice.

Other hands helped her to her feet and flung a blanket around her shoulders. Someone else brought a thick towel to wrap around Ranger and she relinquished the animal into his care. Although she wasn't sure of his condition, at least his heart was still beating.

'You OK, ma'am?' Mr Holley asked, his weathered face lined with worry.

'I'm fine.' She looked at Peter, who was intent on removing Billy's wet coat.

What had once been a quiet, peaceful refuge now bustled with activity. Two men rushed Ranger to the vet. Someone else thrust a cup of hot coffee into her hands. She clutched the mug, grateful for the warmth as she moved nearer Peter. With the arrival of two emergency service personnel, her assistance wasn't needed.

'How's he doing?' she asked, noting the whitened skin of Billy's wrists, hands and fingers. His shivers and chattering teeth were a good sign. At least he hadn't advanced to severe hypothermia. In those cases individuals had lost their thermo-regulatory mechanisms and required supportive medical care while their core body temperatures were raised.

'Not bad, but I'm concerned about his arms. We need warm water soaks to thaw him out. Luckily, he wasn't exposed for very long.' Peter turned to the paramedic. 'Don't use friction. Rubbing will only damage the tissue more. Has someone notified his parents?'

'They're on their way,' Mr Holley announced.

'We're going to take you to the hospital, Billy. Your hands will feel numb at times, then maybe start to burn. We'll give you something so it won't hurt so bad.'

Billy nodded. 'My dog?'

'He's on his way to the vet's,' Mr Holley told him.

The boy's chin quivered. 'Will he be OK?'

'We hope so,' Peter said. He spoke to the paramedics. 'Transport him.'

The two staff members lifted the stretcher and crossed the terrain to reach their vehicle. Peter examined Libby's hands. Apparently satisfied by their condition, he said, 'I'd like to go with Billy. Can you drive?'

'You bet.'

'Don't worry, Doctor,' Mr Holley said. 'One of us will make sure your family gets home safely.'

Peter kissed her hard and swiftly, before hurrying after his patient.

Kyle approached with Samantha in tow. The eyes of both of them were wide with concern. 'Mom? Are you all right?' he asked.

Libby crouched down to hug both of them. 'Yes, I am.'

'Why did the little boy go on the lake?' Sam asked.

'His dog ran ahead and, being a puppy, he didn't listen when Billy called him to come back. So Billy tried to get him. The ice broke, the dog fell in and that's apparently when you two heard him yelling for help.'

'Then we saved his life?' Sam asked.

Libby nodded. 'I'd say so.'

Sam and Kyle stared at each other. Their mouths stretched into huge grins and the two gave each other a clap of victory high above their heads.

As if she realized an important person was missing from their celebration, Sam looked in all directions. 'Where's my dad?'

'He's riding back to town in the ambulance. They're going to the hospital.'

'Oh.' A second later dismay flooded Sam's elfin features. 'We didn't get our tree.'

'Another day, sweetheart.'

'But I found the one I wanted. If we wait someone else might take it.'

Fatigue and the cold lapped at the edges of Libby's strength, yet she hated to disappoint Sam. She groaned inwardly at the prospect of trudging after the dropped hacksaw and her Thermos.

Mr Holley came near. 'Why the sad face, honey?'

Sam's lower lip jutted out. 'We have to go. Me and my dad didn't get our tree.'

'We'll get it, but first I have to find the saw we left by the walnut grove,' Libby said.

'Well, now,' Mr Holley said, 'don't worry about a thing. I'll send someone after it.' He spoke to one of the men, who set off in the direction of their rest area. 'Which one did you pick?'

Sam pointed. A tree only a few feet away had a pink facial tissue twisted around the tip of a lower branch. 'That's mine.'

Mr Holley stared at the pine for a long minute. The crowning branch was crooked and the whole tree had a windswept appearance. 'You're sure?'

Sam's head bobbed up and down.

He glanced at Libby. She shrugged.

'I want it 'cos no one else will,' Sam said, folding her arms across her chest.

Kyle walked around the tree and stood near Libby. 'One side looks pretty good.'

Too tired to argue, Libby turned to Mr Holley. 'We'll take it.'

Obviously bewildered, he placed the saw blade against the trunk and soon wood chips began to fly. A short time later the medium-sized evergreen joined the other in the bed of the pickup.

Mr Holley brushed aside all efforts to pay him. 'Billy wanders over here a lot and helps me out with little jobs. Can't imagine not seeing that boy again. I'm grateful you folks rescued him.'

'Me too.'

After warming themselves by the bonfire and finishing off the last of the cider, thanks to the man who'd found her Thermos, Libby and her tired group crawled into Eldon's pickup. Before they'd driven more than a few miles both Sam and Kyle were sound asleep.

Once they arrived home Libby sawed off a few inches on each trunk and stood the trees in buckets of water. As she finished a car stopped at the curb and Peter stepped out. With purposeful strides and his gaze trained on her, he walked a straight line across the snow-covered lawn.

Her exhaustion suddenly vanished. Before she could welcome him his arms opened wide. In the next instant she found herself enfolded in his tight embrace.

# CHAPTER SEVEN

ALTHOUGH Peter knew in his mind that Libby was safe, he needed the reassurance of her warm presence. He rested his chin on the top of her head, breathing in the combination of her familiar scent and the tangy odor of pine.

'We're on display,' she said.

'Who cares?' he asked, making no effort to release her. He could easily imagine the neighbors' reactions, especially Sylvia's and Ralph's. The older woman had sung Libby's praises during their Thanksgiving dinner and her attempt at matchmaking hadn't been subtle.

'What's the hug for?'

'You're safe and sound,' he said, his voice hoarse. Once he'd dealt with the emergency he realized how easily she could have joined Billy's dog. It was a thought guaranteed to produce nightmares.

'Of course.' She wrapped her hands around his back. 'I was so worried about you.'

'Eldon's pickup *is* bigger than my car, but I managed—'

'Not about driving. About being on the frozen lake. All I could see in my mind was the ice breaking and you falling through.'

'I didn't.'

'Thank God.' His prayer was fervent.

'Now you know how I felt, watching you.'

He wore a wry grin. 'I suppose.' Keeping his arm around her, he guided her inside the garage. 'We make a great team, don't we?'

Her smile warmed his heart. 'How's Billy?'

'Recovering. His fingers are the worst. There's some swelling, but we have the pain under control. I noticed some blistering so we'll keep those debrided and use a topical aloe vera gel every few hours. To be on the safe side, he's getting penicillin, ibuprofen to decrease platelet clumping and a prophylactic tetanus injection. His electrolyte levels are good, which is another point in his favor. By the way, Billy's parents asked for your name. They want to thank you in person.'

She grinned. 'Any news about the dog?'

'The vet called right before I left the hospital. For now, Ranger is holding his own.'

'Billy will be crushed if his pet doesn't make it.'

'I know. Billy insisted he has to get better so he can take care of him.' He pointed to the buckets. 'So you found Sam a tree?'

'I suggested we wait, but since she'd chosen it before the lake episode Mr Holley cut it for us.'

'I suppose the next thing on the agenda is to buy all the trimmings.'

'Unless she wants to make them with us.'

Her comment reminded him of their limited finances. Their old coats, the dated style of her dinette set and the cheaply made bedroom furniture had all pointed to frugal living. The blanket throws over the sofa and chairs lent a homey air to the living room, but they were probably intended to hide years of wear and tear.

He also understood why she'd volunteered to work a friend's shift on the night of St Nick's Christmas bash. She needed the money for more important things—like Kyle's presents—than a cocktail dress. Although he would have enjoyed partying for the first time in several years, he hadn't attended. He'd only wanted to accom-

pany Libby—no other woman would have done—and
he'd refused to go alone.

'What would we need?' he asked. In retrospect, he
wished that he'd paid for the cookie ingredients since
he'd brought home dozens for his freezer.

'I should have everything, but if you want to bring
extra construction paper, glue and glitter that would be
great. Kyle and I will start working tomorrow night. It
usually takes a week since we only devote a few hours
an evening to our project. School comes first.'

Peter mentally reviewed his calendar. To his delight,
his evenings were free—and he knew where he'd like
to spend them. Considering how Sam had hinted about
being part of Libby's family, his daughter wouldn't
debate her decision for long, if at all. 'I'll ask her, but
I can guess which option she'll choose.'

She raised one eyebrow. 'Oh?'

He nodded. 'Your place. From the things she's said,
she'd be your shadow if I let her.'

Her face turned pink. 'It's all part of the service of
making this Christmas special.'

'And what about when the season is over?' he asked,
hiding his apprehension under a light tone. The hours
shared with Libby and Kyle reminded him of the family
unit he'd never created with Carol. Now he wanted it
with his whole heart. And he wanted it with Libby.

If he hadn't been watching her reaction he would
have missed seeing her stiffen. Before he could ponder
its meaning she resumed her carefree attitude.

'I don't make plans for after Christmas until after
Christmas. Who knows what can happen?'

He recognized her stalling tactic and decided not to
press the point. After all, Libby was right. Who knew
what would happen, especially with Kyle and Sam act-

ing as eager accomplices? 'By the way,' he said, 'what does Kyle want for Christmas?'

'A bicycle, among other things.'

'Is there a chance his dad will buy one?'

Libby scoffed. 'His father has never laid eyes on him, much less bought him a present.'

Although he wondered at the reasons, an absent father wasn't uncommon. All things considered, the arrangement should work to his advantage. *He* wanted to step into the shoes of Kyle's father, and with this man off the scene he wouldn't have to overcome any opposition.

Shortly after Kyle had been tucked into bed that same evening, Libby heard a brisk rap at the back door. Recognizing Sylvia's knock, Libby crossed the kitchen and welcomed her neighbor. Sylvia bustled in, garbed to the teeth in winter clothing.

'I came to see how your day went,' the older woman said, turning down her collar before she unzipped her jacket and draped it over a chair.

'You didn't need to brave the cold to ask,' Libby chided. 'There's always the phone.'

Sylvia pulled a chair away from the kitchen table and sank into it. 'I didn't want to wake Kyle. Besides, it's nice to have a change in scenery. Now, tell me how the day went,' she repeated.

'I will,' Libby promised as she poured another cup of coffee and placed it in front of her guest. 'But first I want the scoop on this budding romance between you and Ralph.'

Sylvia's face colored. 'We patched up an old quarrel, that's all.'

'Must have been some quarrel.'

Sylvia clasped the mug with both hands. 'Years ago he asked me to marry him. I refused.'

'No kidding?'

'He was quite a rabble-rouser in those days. Never could seem to settle down in one job. My dad was that way and, believe me, while he was between his so-called business opportunities times were tough.'

'And you didn't want that lifestyle.'

'No, I didn't. Of course, Ralph never understood. We always had fun together and he could make me laugh, but I wanted security.'

'So you said no.'

Sylvia's shoulders heaved. 'I married another young man from school. He was exactly what I wanted—a stable family man, a good provider. We moved away and had thirty-two wonderful years together. I'm not bragging, but he made sure I'd be financially able to take care of myself if it should become necessary. Unfortunately, it did.'

'And Ralph?'

'As you know, he married too. Shortly afterwards he went into the bricklaying business with his father. Stayed in Belleville his whole life.'

Now the animosity and the verbal digs Ralph paid Sylvia made sense. 'So how did you straighten out the hard feelings between you?'

Sylvia leaned closer in a conspiratorial whisper. 'I've tried to talk to him for years, but he'd always walk away. With his broken leg, I had a captive audience. He had no choice but to listen.'

Her satisfied smile hinted that she hadn't finished the tale. Libby guessed at the ending. 'I assume one of you will be selling your house and moving?'

'We're talking about it,' Sylvia admitted. 'But I don't feel right about marrying him when his own child is at odds with him. We've resolved our differences—now I want him to restore his relationship with his son. Ralph needs more than his leg healed this holiday season.'

Libby noticed a gleam in her neighbor's eyes. 'I assume you have an idea?'

'Yes, but I don't have all the details worked out yet. I do know this—I'll have to arrange a meeting before Ralph's casts come off in a few weeks.'

'Still aiming for a captive audience?'

'It worked for me. It's bound to work between Ralph and his son.'

'Whatever you decide, count me in, partner.'

'Good.' Sylvia rested her elbows on the table and leaned forward. 'Now it's your turn.'

'Samantha and Kyle found the trees they wanted. We ran into some excitement, though.' Libby explained about the lake incident.

By the time she'd finished her tale Sylvia's eyes were saucer-sized. 'Thank goodness you saved the boy,' she said. 'Can you imagine how his parents would feel?'

'More than you'll ever know,' Libby answered. If she ever lost Kyle. . . She shuddered.

'And how did you and Peter get along?' Sylvia wiggled her eyebrows.

Thinking of their kiss under the trees, heat surged into Libby's face. She sipped her lukewarm coffee. 'Fine.'

'He needs a wife. His daughter also needs a woman's influence.'

'As far as I can see, Peter's managing on his own. Between Mrs Bridges and Sam's second-grade teacher, Sam has plenty of female attention.'

'Come, now,' Sylvia tutted. 'Do you honestly believe the housekeeper or a woman with twenty other eight-year-olds can fill a mother's shoes?'

'No, but I can't take care of every motherless child.'

'I didn't say you should. Just Samantha.'

Libby gritted her teeth. First it was Kyle, now Sylvia.

Even Peter had alluded to a future. It was easy to buy into the concept that they were two single parents who shared their children's interests and had formed a personal attachment in the process. But they weren't two single parents who'd met a few weeks ago. Their past lay between them like a deep chasm. It could never be crossed, no matter how much she pretended otherwise.

'Out of the question,' Libby said flatly.

Sylvia's eyes narrowed. 'I thought you liked the little girl.'

'I do.'

'Then what's the problem?'

'Extenuating circumstances.' Libby clamped her jaw shut.

As if Sylvia knew Libby wouldn't explain, she tried a new tack. 'What about Kyle? The way his eyes follow Peter whenever he's nearby just about breaks my heart. The boy needs a father. You can't find a more perfect candidate than Peter Caldwell.'

Libby ran her finger along the top of her coffee-mug. Deep down she agreed, but her mind counted off all the reasons why it was impossible.

'Is it because he's Kyle's relative?'

Libby jostled her cup, sloshing coffee onto the table. 'What makes you say that?'

'I may wear bifocals but I'm not blind. You only have to look at the two of them—actually, the three of them—to see the family resemblance.'

Libby's stomach somersaulted. If Sylvia had noticed the similarities, would Peter? And, if so, when?

Sylvia studied Libby. 'Since Peter didn't know you when he moved to town I doubt he's the father. Uncle, perhaps?'

Libby shook her head. 'A cousin of some sort. Kyle's father and Peter were—are—cousins. Their dads were

twins, which explains why Kyle could easily pass for
Peter's son.'

'Will you tell Peter?'

'Absolutely not.' Her answer was vehement.

'If something develops between you two he'll have
to know. . .'

'Nothing will develop. I won't let it.'

Sylvia's forehead wrinkled and she wore a puzzled
frown. 'Why not?'

'Bryce—Kyle's father,' she clarified, 'knew my
sister was pregnant. He refused all help other than to
give her money for an abortion. Peter acted as go-
between.'

'Oh, dear,' Sylvia said, dismayed.

'The Caldwell family officially rejected Kyle. They
don't belong in his life now. They don't deserve the
privilege.'

Sylvia rose to refill her mug. 'Maybe not, but you
can't function as judge and jury. Besides, Peter knows
Kyle and, to state the obvious, he likes him. He won't
hurt the boy. Tell him the truth. Let him decide.'

'Suppose I do follow your advice? Peter will pass
the news on to his cousin. How do you think Bryce
will react? The man has three daughters. He'll be
delighted to hear about a son. Do you honestly believe
he won't fight me for custody?'

Sylvia hesitated. 'It's possible, I suppose.'

Now that Libby had voiced her worries, they tumbled
out of her mouth like water from a broken faucet.
'Where will Peter be in the middle of this mess? Do
you think he'll support me—or his cousin?'

'You're not giving him the benefit of the doubt.'

'I can't afford to,' Libby said, her tone flat. 'I won't
lose my son. That's why Bryce's name isn't listed on
Kyle's birth certificate.'

'I'm not familiar with all the science nowadays, but isn't there a DNA test that's practically foolproof? Seems to me that if Kyle's father wanted to fight you it wouldn't matter that his name wasn't on some piece of paper.'

'I'll deal with that when the time comes.'

'I hope you know what you're doing. If Peter finds out from someone other than you he'll feel betrayed, just like he did with his wife.'

'I know.' Sadness filled Libby's heart. 'But I can't betray my sister, or Kyle either.'

Ten days later, Libby reported to her new assignment— the nursery. At least twelve bassinets were crowded into the small room and most of their occupants were awake.

'I see business is booming,' she commented to the nurse who was changing a wet diaper. 'Sounds like you have a cranky bunch.'

'Don't worry,' Rhonda told her kindly. 'Most of the babies room in with their mothers so you won't see them too often. Several are going home today. Normally I can manage on my own, but we have two infants right now who require most of my attention.'

Rhonda pointed to the two cribs in the isolation room. 'The little one on the left has neonatal sepsis, caused by Group B streptococcus. Her mom's membranes ruptured prematurely—about twelve hours before birth.'

Libby remembered from her training that this particular strain of strep was the most common cause of sepsis in neonates, probably because the organism often inhabited the mother's birth canal.

'My other fellow, Baby Boy Paulsen, is withdrawing from cocaine, thanks to his mother. His drug screen is positive.' She shook her head. 'I'd like to do bodily injury to that woman for what she's done to this poor child.'

Libby peered at the tiny infant who, even in his sleep, seemed restless. His little face wrinkled occasionally as if he wanted to scream his displeasure but was too tired to do so.

'She claims she hasn't used anything during her pregnancy. Supposedly she wanted to avoid drugs during delivery so she decided to indulge herself when her labor started.' The distaste on Rhonda's face was obvious.

'Do you think she's telling the truth?'

'I'm not inclined to believe her,' Rhonda said honestly. 'His weight is low—barely over five pounds—and his Apgar score was seven, rather than the nine or ten I see in healthy babies. Thanks to the phenobarbital, his symptoms are mild—restlessness, irritability, some vomiting. If we feed him every few hours and keep him swaddled he does fairly well, but it's hard to guess at the long-term effects. I cuddle him every chance I get. He seems to like it.'

'I thought more expectant mothers were realizing how drugs harmed their babies.'

'There's no excuse if they don't,' Rhonda said. 'Between public service announcements on television and radio, pamphlets in doctors' offices, the health department, and in the schools, a person would have to be living on another planet not to hear the message. Have you seen the special baby bottle we have on the floor?'

Libby shook her head.

'We bought it from one of our suppliers. It's a clear bottle, filled with a solidified gel. Cigarette butts, beer bottle caps, pills—everything you can imagine—are suspended inside. We show it to all the Lamaze classes during their tour of our facility. There's a note attached to the effect that you wouldn't feed these things to your baby after he was born so don't feed them to him beforehand. It helps get the point across.'

'Obviously Crystal Paulsen didn't take the tour.'

'Obviously not. Rumor says she intends to sign him over for adoption as she's not married. For his sake, I hope she does.' Rhonda sighed. 'Anyway, you've been here before and know the routine. If you need help just yell.'

One by one Libby dealt with her charges, starting with the young lady who was screaming the loudest. After she was dry and wrapped snugly in a blanket with a pacifier in her mouth she settled down.

For the next few hours Libby spent her time feeding, changing and delivering her tiny bundles to waiting parents.

In between, she dealt with lab technicians who drew blood for bilirubin levels and blood counts, reducing her sleepy and contented patients to teary wakefulness.

After the last one had been consoled Libby made herself comfortable in the wooden rocking chair and prepared to bottle-feed the most precious baby girl she'd ever seen.

Wisps of tawny hair clung to a perfectly shaped head. Rosebud lips puckered and held the nipple firmly. Dark eyes stared at Libby with interest and one tiny hand wrapped around Libby's little finger.

'Oh, Mandy,' Libby crooned. 'You're a sweetheart, aren't you?'

Baby formula bubbled around Mandy's mouth and she smiled, before giving a loud burp. Libby raised her to her shoulder and rubbed her tiny back to bring up more air.

'I see you've latched onto my favorite patient,' Peter announced from the doorway.

'I can't believe she's real. She hardly makes any fuss. I've never seen a baby with such a placid personality. Even asleep, Kyle was always in motion. I savored those times when he wanted to snuggle.'

Mandy gave a contented sigh and her eyelids drifted closed. Reluctant to return Mandy to her bed, Libby decided to indulge herself for a few more minutes.

'You should have had more children.'

'It takes two.'

'You're young. There's still time.'

If I had a husband, she thought. Instead of answering, she rose and strode toward Mandy's crib, conscious of Peter's gaze following her movements.

'You have a nice touch,' he commented as she tucked Mandy in her bassinet.

She stroked the baby's downy face and patted the little rump stuck in the air. 'Thanks. Now that she's asleep I suppose you want to wake her,' she grumbled without malice.

He grinned. 'How's she doing?'

'Gaining weight. Her vital signs and lab work are normal.'

'I'll catch her on my next trip through. Right now, I want to check out this little guy.' He strode toward the Paulsen baby's crib. As Peter unwrapped the blanket around the tiny form arms and legs kicked in startled motions. His wizened face wrinkled with displeasure and he bellowed a howl of distress.

Standing next to Peter, Libby stroked the baby's arms. 'Now, Ty, don't wake everyone up. I'll hold you as soon as we're finished.'

Ty's cries grew louder as Peter placed a stethoscope on his tiny chest. 'So his mother's decided on a name?'

'No. I refuse to call him "baby" until his mama makes up her mind so I picked one out myself.'

'It suits him,' Peter said, checking Ty's reflexes and responses to stimuli.

'I thought so.'

Peter straightened. 'All done. Apparently the phenobarbital is controlling his withdrawal symptoms.'

'How long will he have to take the medication?' she asked as she deftly rewrapped Ty in a blanket.

'I'll start tapering the dose until he's completely off. A few weeks at the most.' He watched her quietly for several minutes. 'Have you always wanted to be a nurse?'

His change in topic caught her by surprise. 'My goal was to be a doctor. Unfortunately, life didn't go as I'd planned.' She cradled Ty in her left arm. 'What about you?'

'I'd considered a career in medicine, but my father steered me toward business.'

'What made you decide to enter health care?'

He paused for several seconds. 'The turning point came after I'd advised a young woman to get an abortion.'

Libby's heart skipped a beat. She clutched Ty tightly to her chest until he squeaked in protest. 'Did you have a good reason for doing so?' Holding her breath, she sat down to wait for his reply.

He shook his head. 'Strictly for convenience's sake. My cousin, who was like a brother, became involved with a college student. Considering that both of their futures were at stake, it seemed the best solution. As time went on I saw there were other, less permanent solutions. Eventually I regretted the part I'd played.'

'Maybe the girl didn't take your advice,' Libby said, testing his reaction.

'She did,' he said flatly. 'I saw the doctor's bill for services rendered.'

'How did your cousin feel after that?'

'We both went out and got drunk. Not a very mature thing to do, I know. After that he wasn't the same—more serious, less fun-loving. I think he wished he'd made another choice.' He paused. 'As for myself, I wished I'd done as she'd begged—asked him to reconsider.'

Libby clamped her teeth together to keep from blurting out the truth. The secret had to remain—Peter's honesty confirmed her fears.

Bryce would want his son.

If Peter realized that Kyle was that child she'd face more legal problems than she could possibly imagine. Her hand shook as she absent-mindedly smoothed down the spiky strands of Ty's blond hair.

Peter straightened, curving his mouth into a slight smile. 'Now you've heard my darkest secrets.'

'I guess so.'

He studied her face and frowned. 'You're looking a little green. Are you OK?'

'I'm fine,' she insisted, ignoring the tight band of despair clamped around her chest. 'The busy morning is catching up on me. I just need my second wind.'

'Maybe this Christmas thing is wearing you out. We decorated our yards, our houses, our trees. Last night we went ice skating. The night before we caroled at the nursing home with the church youth group. It's time we spent a quiet evening together.'

'And listen to two kids whine all night because they didn't go to the Elf's Workshop?' She shook her head. 'Not a chance. After a cup of coffee I'll be fine.'

He didn't appear convinced. 'Well, *I* wouldn't mind a break in the action. Why don't we just wander around town, look at the Christmas lights and then go home?'

'Suits me. Provided you can persuade the two young-sters to change their plans.'

'Leave everything to me,' he said. 'Barring any emer-gency, Sam and I will drop by your house around seven o'clock.'

Once he'd left Libby continued to rock Ty in silence. Her thoughts tumbled end over end in her mind.

Over the past few weeks her first impression of Peter being a cold-hearted man had wavered but hadn't changed completely. Now, with the baring of his soul, she couldn't cling to her misconceptions any longer. In his own way, he'd been affected by those previous events. Perhaps not to the extent she and Elaine had, but Elaine's pregnancy had changed his life nonetheless.

In that instant all her vows to keep an emotional distance from Peter crumbled into dust. In spite of her intentions, her personal assurances, she had done the unthinkable.

She'd fallen in love with Peter Caldwell.

Sylvia's admonitions echoed as clearly as if she'd spoken them in that instant. The clock ticked closer to the time of Libby's reckoning. Yet no matter how she looked at the situation, if Peter ever discovered the truth the outcome was the same. She'd lose both him and Kyle.

For her sake and Kyle's the boy's true parentage must remain a secret. To some, her decision would not seem right. But, like the one she'd made ten years ago, it was the only one she could live with.

Later that evening, after they'd spent hours driving around Belleville and exclaiming over twinkling lights of every size, shape and color and Kyle and Sam were asleep, dreaming of sleighs, Santa Claus, reindeer and presents, Peter knocked on Libby's door.

His serious expression sent a foreboding chill through her. She ushered him inside. 'What's wrong? Where's Sam?'

'I have a young neighbor babysitting.' He sat on the sofa. 'I'm not a particularly patient man. I'd planned on waiting a while before I brought up the subject, but I want this out in the open.'

The feeling of impending doom spread, courtesy of her guilty conscience. Her hand flew to her throat. 'What is it?'

'I want us to be a family.'

Of all the topics he could have mentioned, this one hadn't crossed her mind. 'You...do?'

He nodded. 'I love Kyle and I love you. Sam does, too. There's no need for either of us to be alone.'

Tears came to her eyes. 'I don't know what to say.'

'Say yes.'

'I'd love to, but...'

'But what?'

She fingered the frayed edge of her shirt-sleeve. 'There are too many things in my past that I can't talk about,' she finished.

'I'm not concerned about the past. Only the future. *Our* future.'

'You say that now, but—'

Peter enfolded her hands in his. 'It's true. The past is gone. Over and done with. It doesn't matter. We can't change anything so let it lie.'

She stared into his eyes. 'If only I could,' she whispered.

'You can and you will.'

His assurance made her smile. 'Such confidence.'

He grinned. 'I have plenty to go around.'

The opportunity to fulfill her dreams was too good

to be true. She wanted to seize the moment and grasp what he offered, but at the same time she was scared to death.

'I love you both, more than I ever imagined. I'd like to say yes, but I need time,' she said apologetically.

He spoke decisively. 'You have until Christmas.'

'Why Christmas?'

'Because I saw Sam's and Kyle's letters to Santa Claus. Your name and mine are top on their list.'


'You're looking extremely happy these days,' Joni said as they waited near the bank of elevators at the end of their shift. She winked. 'Could it have anything to do with a certain doctor?'

Libby grinned. 'It might.'

'I knew it!'

'Then again,' Libby continued, 'it could be because Kathy Sanders was discharged today.' The warm glow she'd felt at both Kathy's and her sister's effusive thanks would remain for some time.

'Oh, yes, the woman with DIC. She was a lucky girl.'

'Definitely. How's Billy Corbett?'

'He's going home tomorrow. His hands will probably be extremely cold-sensitive and he'll have to be very careful when he's outdoors but, considering the alternatives, it's a minor after-effect.'

'Joni!' Both Libby and Joni glanced down the hall at the rapidly advancing ward clerk. 'Telephone.'

'Shoot!' Joni grumbled.

'Want me to hold the elevator?'

'Better not. Who knows how long I'll be? See you later.'

Joni left. Just as Libby decided to take the stairs the elevator arrived. Seeing Peter inside, she gave him a huge smile.

'Feeling brave?' he asked, amused.

She stepped on. 'Nothing like living life on the edge.'

The doors slid shut. He pulled her into his arms. 'How about a dose of moral support?'

'Any time,' she said, reveling in their embrace. 'I hope no one else wants on.'

His 'me, too' was fervent. 'Dare I assume you're getting used to the idea we discussed a few nights ago?'

She moved away to gaze into his eyes. 'Actually, I'm looking forward to it.'

'Maybe we should make our announcement sooner?'

'No.' Libby shook her head for emphasis. 'This is part of the kids' Christmas wish. We can wait another two weeks or so.'

With her arms wrapped around him, she felt the sigh come out of his chest. 'Shall we set a date? The first of the year?'

'That doesn't give us much time to prepare.'

'What's to prepare? We find a minister, order a cake, invite a few friends to my house.'

Libby pictured herself coming down Peter's staircase in a gown of ivory satin. It would be a while until she could afford such a creation. 'I still need more time.'

'How much more?'

'I don't know, but I won't make you wait long. I promise.'

The elevator jolted to a stop. Libby reluctantly dropped her hands to her side. 'Short trip.'

'Yeah. Too bad there aren't eight floors to ground level instead of four.' He reached over her shoulder to depress the 'Close Doors' button and shield them from interested bystanders. 'When can I see you again?'

She grinned. 'When do you want to?'

'Now that's a loaded question. Mrs Bridges is fixing

a pot of beef stew. Why not come over for supper? I should be home by six-thirty.'

'We'll be there.'

His kiss was slow and full of promise. 'Do you have any idea how hard it is to romance someone when you're either at work or surrounded by kids?'

'I certainly do.' Her voice sounded low and sultry.

A few seconds later he took his finger off the button. 'Don't be late.'

To Libby's relief, the hallway outside was vacant. After a polite, 'Goodbye, Dr Caldwell' for the benefit of a chance bystander, she hurried across the street to her car and drove to her doctor's appointment.

The sun shone as brightly as her mood. The temperature was warmer today—mid-fifties—and only a few traces of snow lingered in shaded areas. Libby arrived on time for her annual check-up and a prescription refill. The pills she took alleviated her menstrual cramps, but she hoped she wouldn't be taking them for much longer. She'd welcome another child like Samantha or Kyle.

Pronounced fit a half-hour later, Libby drove home. Since Sylvia had volunteered to babysit Kyle after school, Libby found Sam and Kyle playing in her neighbor's yard.

'Can I go to Sam's house?' Kyle asked as soon as she parked the car. 'There's something we have to do.'

'What?'

'Can't tell,' Samantha said. 'It's a surprise.'

Libby smiled. 'Kyle has to change clothes first.'

He complied in record time, then headed outside. 'Bye, Mom.' Libby took advantage of his absence to call the phone number she'd circled in the previous day's newspaper.

'Yes, ma'am, you're in luck. I have a red bicycle in

the size you want,' the man said. 'It'll be ready by the end of the week.'

'I'll take it.' The price he quoted was a little less than she'd expected, which was welcome news. A reconditioned bicycle was better than nothing, and Kyle would never be able to tell the difference.

Libby replaced the receiver, pleased to give Kyle the number one gift on his list. She sat on the sofa to read the evening newspaper, but before she finished scanning the headlines she heard screams. Frantic screams.

Jumping to her feet, she poked her head outside. Samantha skidded to a stop near the bottom step.

'Gotta come quick,' she panted. 'Kyle fell off his bike. He won't wake up.'

# CHAPTER EIGHT

'WHERE?' Libby demanded.

'In front of my house,' Samantha said.

Libby rushed down the cement stairs and raced to the sidewalk. Ahead, in the direction of the Caldwell home, she saw Kyle. He lay motionless in a tangled heap of metal and twisted bicycle wheels.

She sprinted forward, anxious to reach him and yet scared at what she would find. The sight of Mrs Bridges hovering over him was somewhat comforting—until she saw the worried expression on the elderly woman's face.

'I don't know what happened,' Mrs Bridges said. 'Sam was outside waiting for him and next thing I know she's screaming. I took one look and sent her after you.'

After untangling the broken bicycle from around his legs, Libby knelt beside Kyle. She forced away her maternal bias and studied him with an objective nurse's eye.

'Kyle? Can you hear me, honey?'

He didn't move.

A purplish bruise and lump had formed in the middle of his forehead, obviously the cause of his unconscious state. His face was white and one cheek had bits of dirt imbedded in the scrapes. She took one look at the blood running down his leg from a gash above the right knee. Already his jeans were soaked with the dark red fluid.

'Go inside and call 911,' she instructed Mrs Bridges. 'Tell them we need an ambulance. A possible head injury.'

The housekeeper bustled off. 'Find a towel to wrap around his leg,' she told Samantha.

Without a word, Sam disappeared. The slam of the door sounded like a pistol shot in the late afternoon, but Kyle didn't respond.

Libby examined Kyle's wound. The edges were jagged and the cut itself was deep but, even so, the amount of blood flowing out seemed excessive. 'Kyle? Mom's here. You're going to be fine but you have to wake up.'

The door slammed again. Sam ran toward her, a white towel flying behind her like a cape. 'Here!' she said breathlessly, thrusting the fabric into Libby's hands.

By the time Libby had wrapped his knee a police car and an ambulance had arrived. The two uniformed paramedics brought their carryall while the officer directed traffic and held off the curiosity-seekers.

'He's been unconscious for about ten minutes,' Libby reported as she moved aside so the men could work.

While one took his vital signs, the other retrieved a neck brace, a backboard and a stretcher from the ambulance.

Although as a nurse Libby knew the immobilization measures to Kyle's head and neck were precautionary, the sight of her unconscious son strapped to the backboard was heart-wrenching. The white towel, now stained with blood, was equally troubling. She stood to one side, rubbing her arms.

Sylvia came running. 'Gracious me! How is he?'

'I don't know,' Libby answered. Her voice caught in her throat.

Sylvia hugged her. 'I'm sure he'll be fine. He's a tough little boy.'

'I know.'

The two paramedics lifted the stretcher and carefully

walked to the open ambulance doors. Libby hurried forward. 'May I go with you? I'd like to be with Kyle when he regains consciousness.'

One paramedic started to shake his head but his gaze landed on her uniform and hospital nametag. 'We're not supposed to take riders—legal issues, you know. But since you're a nurse I think we can squeeze you inside. Hop in.'

Libby climbed aboard and the paramedic followed. 'Do you want someone to notify your family physician?' he asked.

'Please. Dr Caldwell.'

The second EMT slammed the double doors closed. While the ambulance slowly rolled down the street with its siren blaring, the other spoke to the emergency room staff on the radio.

Libby fixed her gaze on Kyle. Before they arrived at the ER entrance his eyelids flickered. Tears of relief came to her own eyes. 'Kyle? Can you hear me?'

'Mom?' His voice was weak. 'What. . .happened?'

'You had an accident. You're in an ambulance and we're almost at the hospital.'

Kyle's eyes drifted shut as the vehicle braked to a gentle stop.

The paramedic depressed the doorhandles and jumped out just as the driver came to assist. Thanks to the rollers on the guiding tracks, they pulled the stretcher forward in a smooth motion. Libby hopped onto the concrete while they locked the folding wheel mechanism in place.

Peter and two nurses met them at the automatic doors. Peter's familiar face sent relief humming through her soul.

'What happened?' he asked.

'A bicycle accident,' she reported, struggling to use

her nurse's objectivity. The paramedics recited their findings as they wheeled Kyle into the trauma room.

'Hi, son,' Peter said to Kyle. 'Popping wheelies on your bike again?'

Kyle grimaced. 'Yeah.'

Peter flicked a light across Kyle's eyes to check his pupillary reaction. 'Where does it hurt?'

'My. . .head. My knee.'

Moving to the blood-soaked towel, he called out his orders to the two nurses hovering nearby. 'C-spine X-rays, a CT scan of the skull, CBC and a chem-7.' He undid the crude bandage and frowned. 'I also want coagulation studies: a prothrombin time, PTT and a bleeding time.'

He bent over Kyle. 'We're going to do a lot of different things, but don't be scared. They're not going to hurt. I'll be with you.'

'Where's. . .my. . .mom?'

Libby stepped forward. 'I'm right here.'

A woman wearing the blue smock of a ward clerk walked in and placed a hand on Libby's arm. 'Could you sign the release forms for us?'

'I don't want to leave him—'

'He'll be fine. Won't you, son?' Peter said, staring down at Kyle. Then he spoke to Libby. 'Grab a cup of coffee while you're at it.'

Libby hesitated. The lady tugged on her arm and motioned to the door. 'Please?'

Giving Kyle one last longing glance, Libby followed the clerk to the check-in desk and signed the required forms. By the time she'd finished a lab technician had come and gone and Kyle was on his way to Radiology.

Too nervous to sit, Libby located a coffee-machine down the hall from ER. To her dismay, she didn't have any money—her purse and coat were at home. She returned to the ER waiting room and mindlessly thumbed through one dog-eared magazine after the other.

Finally, after an interminable wait, Peter appeared. She jumped to her feet and tossed the publication onto the end table. 'How is he? Can I see him?'

Peter hugged her close and guided her toward the sofa in a private corner. 'In a minute,' he said, sitting beside her.

She fired her questions. 'His x-rays?'

'No spinal cord injuries.'

The breath she'd been holding came out as a drawn-out sigh and her shoulders slumped. 'What about his head?'

'He has a mild concussion. The CT scan doesn't show any fractures, but he has a lot of superficial bleeding from the bump. I'm keeping him for observation.'

'And his leg?'

'I gave him ten stitches.'

'Did he nick an artery or something? There was so much blood.'

'Actually, that's another reason why I'm admitting him. There shouldn't be as much bleeding as there is for his particular injury. That's why I requested coagulation tests.' He hesitated. 'His results are abnormal.'

Her stomach knotted. 'What do you mean by "abnormal"?'

'His PTT or partial thromboplastin time is prolonged. Usually it's around thirty seconds and Kyle's is forty-eight. His prothrombin time is normal, but his bleeding time is nearly fifteen minutes. The expected result with the method used in our lab is less than four.'

'What are you saying?' Libby's brain seemed to be in a fog as she struggled to sort through her son's problems.

'The bleeding isn't stopping like I'd expect. His results indicate a clotting disorder of some sort,' Peter patiently explained.

'What sort of disorder?'

'I'm not sure, which is why I need to ask you a few more questions. I understand he has a history of epistaxis.' Translating the word to nosebleeds, she nodded and he continued. 'Have you noticed if he bruises easily?'

'He usually has a bruise somewhere on his body, but most active children do, don't they?'

'Do you have any bleeding problems or are there any in your family?'

'No. None.'

'What about Kyle's father?'

She hesitated. 'I don't know.' Once again she paused. 'What do you suspect?'

'As you know, there are two different pathways involved in the coagulation process. The PT and PTT tests screen those pathways. Since Kyle's prothrombin time is normal and his PTT isn't, the problem apparently lies with a protein in only one of the pathways. Of those, factor VIII is the one most commonly affected so I've requested an assay to determine how much factor VIII Kyle actually has.'

Horror struck her. 'You think he's a hemophiliac?'

'That's one of our choices. The other consideration is von Willebrand's disease.'

Libby's heart sank.

'There are two types of haemophilia, A and B, but I doubt Kyle has either one. He would have experienced problems before now. On the other hand, people with mild forms of von Willebrand's often never learn of their condition until they have surgery or suffer an injury.

'In any event, we're performing a number of other blood tests which will differentiate between the two conditions—a von Willebrand factor assay, a ristocetin cofactor assay, platelet aggregation studies. The list goes on. It will take several days for the reports to filter back because our lab sends those samples to a reference facility.'

'And in the meantime?'

'I'll treat him with cryoprecipitate from the blood bank. There's a drug called desmopressin which works well with certain cases of von Willebrand's by causing the endothelial cells to release their stores of von Willebrand factor. Once the factor is in the circulation the platelets will adhere to the injured blood vessel wall and plug the so-called leak. Without this factor the platelets can't function properly and the bleeding continues.'

'So why won't you use the desmopressin now?'

'Because it's only effective against Type I von Willebrand's. If Kyle has one of the other types, or by chance *does* have hemophilia, we could do more harm than good. I don't want to risk it.'

He drew a deep breath. 'I could wait until all the lab results are back but, with the potential for a subdural hematoma from the bump on his head, I don't want to.'

'I see,' she said, numb with shock.

Peter reached out and took her hands. 'He'll be fine. A diagnosis of von Willebrand's isn't a death sentence. Although it's hereditary and only requires one parent to pass the gene along, many people live normal, healthy lives. I know not just from my medical experience but from firsthand knowledge. My cousin, Bryce, and his mother have the condition. Having surgery or a tooth extracted requires advance planning, but the rest of the time they don't need any special attention.'

He rose. 'Come on. Kyle's probably settled in a room upstairs and is wondering where you are.'

Libby stood, trying to assimilate the information she'd been given. Even without the test results, she knew Kyle's condition was the one plaguing the Caldwell line. One more clue about Kyle's identity had been revealed. It was only a matter of time before Peter added them all together and arrived at the conclusion she didn't want him to reach.

Peter flung his arm around her shoulders and led her to the elevator. Once inside, he held her against his chest as he pressed the fourth floor button. 'It's nearly eight o'clock. Did you eat something?'

She shook her head. 'I rode in the ambulance. My purse is at home.'

He swore and moved to send the elevator to the basement cafeteria. She forestalled him by grasping his wrist. 'I can't eat now, anyway. Maybe later.'

His hand dropped. The elevator continued to the fourth floor and the pediatric wing. Outside Kyle's semi-private room Libby stopped to draw a bolstering breath.

Peter squeezed her to give moral support. 'He'll be fine. Don't worry.'

She gave him a tremulous smile, nodded and then stiffened her spine. 'I won't.' Pasting a huge smile on her face, she greeted her son.

'I've been waiting and waiting for you,' Kyle complained. His forehead was turning black and blue, and the hand with the IV was fastened to a cloth-covered board.

This time her grin was genuine. She crossed the room to stand beside the bed, anxious to touch him and reassure herself that he truly was alive and awake. 'How're you feeling, Kyle?'

'Sleepy. Will you stay with me tonight?' His lower lip quivered.

'I wouldn't consider being anyplace else.' Clutching his good hand to her chest, she bent over to kiss him on his unharmed cheek. As she straightened she brushed an unruly lock of hair off his forehead, taking pains to avoid the painful-looking knot.

Kyle's eyelids drooped. Peter carried a high-backed chair to her and she gratefully sank onto the cushions without removing her fingers from Kyle's grip.

Peter crouched beside her and spoke in a low voice. 'Nursing staff will be in every thirty minutes to monitor him for signs of increasing intracranial pressure. You know what that means.'

'They'll check his vitals, his pupils' reaction to light and his level of consciousness.'

He nodded. 'Keep alert if he acts as if he has a stiff neck, which is an indication of bleeding into the meninges. We'll do another CT scan in the morning. By then we should be seeing results from the cryo.'

'How long will you keep him?'

'Twenty-four to forty-eight hours minimum. After that I'll re-evaluate.' He straightened. 'I'm going home to check on Samantha. I'll be back later. Do you need anything?'

'No, but would you mind calling Sylvia? She was worried about him.'

'I'll phone right away.' He bent down to kiss her.

His tenderness was the balm she needed. But after he left reaction set in. Worry over Kyle and fear over the uncertain future sent tears silently coursing down her face.

After hearing Kyle's latest lab report, Peter replaced the receiver on the phone in his study. Although not all the results were in, they pointed to von Willebrand's.

He sat back in his swivel chair and steepled his fingers as he stared at the lighthouse oil painting on the wall opposite him. A small voice from the doorway interrupted his thoughts.

'I know you're in your thinking chair, Daddy,' Sam said, 'but can I ask you something?'

'Sure, honey.'

She ran in and sat on his lap. 'Will Kyle be home in time for Santa Claus?'

He stroked her hair. 'Christmas is over two weeks away. He'll be home in a few days.'

'Good. I just wondered if we'd have to take his present to his house or to the hospital.'

'We'll take it to his house.' He glanced at the clock on his desk. 'It's nearly nine. You have school tomorrow. Better go to bed.'

'I will. G'night.' She planted a wet kiss on his cheek and he hugged her close.

'Sweet dreams. I'll see you in the morning.'

Sam slid off his lap and skipped out the door.

Peter watched her leave with fondness, wondering how he would have borne up under the news Libby had received. Even so, he felt Libby's pain because Kyle seemed as if he were Peter's own son.

They were a family meant to be together. After all, how many times in their outings had people remarked on how the children resembled him? Kyle's hair color had a lot to do with it, he was sure, but even so the boy had mannerisms that often mirrored his own. Just as Libby had despaired of Kyle's painstaking, near-perfectionist tendencies, he remembered his mother and aunt swapping similar stories about him and Bryce.

What a surprise to discover Kyle had the same medical condition, too. He wondered what the odds were

for a child from a totally different gene pool to have
so much in common with his family.

*Unless he* **wasn't** *from a totally different gene pool.*

The thought came from nowhere. Was it possible?
Peter stiffened. He reached for a note pad and performed
a few calculations.

His final answer leaped off the page. The year of
Kyle's conception was significant—it coincided with
his final year in the University of Kansas's MBA
program.

Thinking back to those days, he remembered the
name of the woman he'd visited. He could see it written
on the envelope he'd handed her. E. Brown. Another
coincidence.

Or was it?

Was Libby another woman entirely, or was 'Libby'
a pet name which she used exclusively?

Was the reason he'd felt an instant kinship with Kyle
because on a subconscious level the boy reminded him
of Bryce—and himself—as a child?

Once Peter questioned the similarities, others came
to mind and fell into place. Libby had been seventeen
when she'd dropped out of school. Using her current
age, he calculated the year. It matched.

Libby had admitted she'd wanted to enter medical
school. She'd had no contact with Kyle's father since
before he was born. The signs all pointed to Libby being
the college student involved with his cousin.

She didn't look anything like the girl he remembered.
While some people didn't change noticeably over the
years others did, and obviously Libby fell in the latter
category.

And yet, he recalled the E. Brown he'd met had
possessed a fiery disposition. The years had obviously
tempered the trait but not erased it. Who else had the

nerve to scold him about Kathy Sanders?

A bitter sense of betrayal filled his mouth. Libby had known who he was from the very beginning. No wonder she'd avoided him. If it hadn't been for Sam, Libby would have remained anonymous—merely another nurse in the crowd.

Sam.

Luckily, they'd kept their future plans a secret. Samantha would be crushed if her hopes had been realized and then dashed, as his now were. Libby's silence had shattered his trust. Thank goodness he'd discovered her secret before it was too late.

'I had Sylvia drop your coat and purse by my house,' Peter said as he carried the articles into Kyle's hospital room and unceremoniously dumped them on another chair.

'Thanks.' Libby pointed to the tray on Kyle's bedside table. 'And thanks for the food. The nurse told me you'd asked the kitchen staff to send sandwiches. It was thoughtful of you.'

She crossed the room to give him a hug, but he held himself stiff. Noticing the lack of emotion on his face, worry flooded her heart. 'What's wrong with Kyle's tests—?'

'The preliminary lab results suggest von Willebrand's. But, after hearing me ramble on about my family, you already know that,' he said sharply.

He knew. *He knew.* She opened her mouth to speak but under his icy gaze, she couldn't. Instead, she turned to study her sleeping son.

'I assume Libby is a nickname.'

She nodded once. 'It's short for Elizabeth.'

'You're the girl I talked to in the dorm.'

He didn't pose questions, only stated facts in the

impersonal tone of an interrogator. 'Yes.'

'You didn't see the doctor.'

She pointed to Kyle. 'It's rather obvious, wouldn't you say?'

'Who did?'

'A girl I knew who found herself in a similar situation.'

'Why the secrecy?'

She stared at him, her mouth agape. 'You can honestly ask that? Bryce threatened to take the baby away if he was ever named as the father or if he' was approached for child support. He wanted an abortion, but it was out of the question. Rather than throw the letter away, I gave it to someone who wanted it.

'Now, if you don't mind,' she said, glowering at him, 'can we continue this some other time? Some other place?'

'The time is now, although I agree we should conduct our discussion in another place. Shall we?' He stepped aside, as if expecting her to precede him.

'I can't leave Kyle alone.'

'He's sleeping. This won't take long.'

The moment of reckoning had come. She squared her shoulders and strode into the hallway.

Peter followed, then increased his strides to pass her. He eventually chose an empty patient room at the opposite end of the paeds unit.

After flicking the switch for the fluorescent lights near the head of the bed, he closed the door. He stood with his feet slightly apart, his arms folded across his chest, his eyes narrowed. 'Why didn't you tell me?'

She stared out the window. The glow of the street-lamps illuminated the sidewalk, and she watched small figures hurry in and out of the building. 'I couldn't.'

'Good God, Libby. I asked you to *marry* me. I deserved to know.'

Anger surged through her like a red-hot current of electricity. She turned. 'What's this about "I'm not concerned about the past. Only the future." and "We can't change anything so let it lie"? Was that just a line?'

'No.'

'Then why are you so upset? Is it because I tried to follow your advice and bury the past, or because Kyle's father is your cousin?'

'You should have told me.'

'When? The first time I saw you in the elevator? When I came to your house about the Christmas competition? Or maybe after you'd asked me to help you make this Christmas special for Samantha?'

'If I recall, I mentioned how badly I felt about encouraging a young woman to have an abortion. That would have been an excellent time to admit you were the girl involved.'

Libby sank onto the bed. The day had held too many shocks and surprises, and she felt utterly drained of every ounce of energy she possessed. 'I couldn't,' she repeated.

'Were you trying to play me for a fool? Have the dubious honor of wrapping two Caldwells around your finger? Or did you have something else in mind? Revenge, perhaps?'

Her eyes burned. She shook her head. 'No. None of those things.'

'Why, Libby? I need to know your reasons.' His tone was pleading, almost begging.

She brushed at the silent tears trickling down her face. 'You'd tell Bryce and he'd take Kyle away from me.'

In the ensuing quiet she heard the distant 'ding' of someone's call bell. 'He has a right to know.'

Libby jumped to her feet. 'No, he doesn't,' she ground out, her entire body stiff and her fists clenched at her side. 'He didn't want a child. If I'd followed his advice—and yours—Bryce wouldn't have the opportunity to change his mind.'

'He regrets his decision.'

Remembering Peter's conversation about Bryce's inner turmoil and the change it had brought to his life, she knew Peter was right.

Unfortunately, Libby wasn't ready to forgive him.

'I'm sure he does but, as far as I'm concerned, it's too late. Bryce Caldwell doesn't have a son,' she said vehemently. '*I* do.'

Peter shook his head. 'Denying it won't change a thing.' He pivoted to leave.

She rushed forward. 'What are you going to do?'

'I intend to follow the same advice I gave you. I'll make the choice I can live with.'

He flung open the door, then hesitated. Before he stepped into the hallway he looked over his shoulder at her. 'For what it's worth, Libby Brown, I'm grateful for the decision you made.'

As he strode away Libby hoped that someday she could respond in kind.

# CHAPTER NINE

LIBBY hurried down the empty corridor to Kyle's room. With her heart aching and her eyes burning, she slipped inside. As she gazed upon her sleeping son and lightly touched his cheek she knew she'd do whatever was necessary to keep him in her care.

She didn't blame Peter for being angry—she'd expected him to react as he had. Perhaps in time he might forgive her, but she thought it unlikely. Although he'd realized who Kyle's father was, he still believed that Libby was his real mother. She should have told him, but at the time she hadn't thought clearly. Withholding the information didn't serve any purpose since Bryce knew the truth.

Sadly, Peter would never see it as anything but another lie of omission.

Throughout the night she dozed in the chair next to Kyle's bed, waking each time the night nurse came in to check on Kyle's condition. Although she was greatly relieved there weren't any signs of a subdural hematoma, her spirits remained as heavy as the darkness surrounding the hospital. Finally, as the bright rays of dawn filtered through the zoo animal curtains, her natural optimism took over and her inner gloom lifted with the hope of a new day.

Surely Peter would understand that her fears had governed her silence. Surely he'd understand that she'd had no other ulterior motive. And surely he'd understand she couldn't have made any other decision under the circumstances.

The moment he made rounds she'd pull him aside and tell him everything. No more secrets.

The breakfast cart rattled off the elevator. The delicious aroma of food wafted into the room and her stomach growled. She slipped into the bathroom, washed the sleep out of her eyes, undid the clip at her nape and combed her hair. Too bad she didn't carry a toothbrush in her purse. Lack of sleep had brought on a headache and she swallowed a few ibuprofen.

By the time she'd finished a lab technician had arrived to take another blood sample.

'You're doing great,' Libby praised Kyle after the phlebotomist had left with his tray of tubes. 'How're you feeling this morning?'

'Better. I'm hungry.'

Peter's comments about hunger being the best sign of a male's recovery came to mind. She grinned. 'I'm sure we'll find something to fill the hole in your stomach.'

The door opened and Joni bustled in, wearing a smock covered with giraffes and elephants. 'Good morning, Kyle. I see you're awake.'

'I'm hungry,' Kyle repeated.

'I'll bring breakfast as soon as I've finished checking you,' Joni said. She spoke to Libby. 'Sounds like you had an interesting evening. You should have called me. I'd have dropped by to lend moral support. You didn't need to face this alone.'

*I didn't*, Libby thought. *Peter was here*. At least for a little while. She cleared her throat. 'Yeah, well, I managed. What time does Dr Caldwell make rounds?'

'In about an hour,' Joni said, flashing a light in Kyle's eyes. 'Dr Caldwell left a note on Kyle's chart that Dr Downey would be taking over this morning as he's back from his cruise. He usually comes in about the same time as Dr Caldwell.'

Her hopes at seeing Peter died. The underlying message was extremely clear—he'd rejected both her and Kyle. Idyllic dreams of a blended family died in an instant. Her throat burned and she tried to swallow.

Joni clicked off her penlight. 'Didn't he tell you?'

Libby averted her gaze. 'I guess I forgot.'

'Well, young man. You're looking good this morning. I'll bet I can find a tray with your name on it.'

'I'm starving,' Kyle said, his eyes bright with anticipation.

'Be right back.' Joni returned with toast and scrambled eggs. 'If you need anything let me know.' She addressed Libby. 'Why don't you run home, shower and change clothes? I'll keep an eye on Kyle so he stays out of trouble.' She winked at him and he grinned.

'Thanks, but I don't have my car here. I'll call my neighbor. She'll bring a fresh outfit. I can shower in the nurses' lounge.'

Joni dug in the pocket of her smock and tossed her a set of keys. 'Don't be silly. You can use the break. Get some fresh air; add color to your cheeks. Kyle can manage for a few hours without you.'

Libby hesitated. 'OK, but I'll be back in thirty minutes.'

'Take your time,' Joni advised. 'If he's not here when you get back he'll be in Radiology.'

Libby rushed home. As she walked in the door the sight of the Christmas tree with the ornaments the four of them had cut, glued, and glittered sent a bittersweet feeling through her. Then anger welled in its place.

How dare Peter claim that he loved her and that he loved Kyle, then deny them so completely!

An unreasonable desire blossomed. She wanted to

throw out the tree and every memory associated with it. The trash service came today—the pine could be gone in a matter of hours. Who cared if the neighbors wondered why a fully decorated tree lay next to the curb with the bags of garbage destined for the landfill? She didn't.

And yet she couldn't follow through with her mental threat. No matter how Peter's rejection had hurt her, Christmas was for kids. Kyle had formed extra-special memories of the holiday this year and she couldn't destroy them. She *wouldn't* destroy them.

She sank onto sofa and smoothed the wrinkles on the cover beside her. Besides, how could she explain her actions? Trying to do so would raise more questions in her son's mind than if she suffered in silence.

Drawing a bracing breath, she rose to shower and change out of the uniform she'd worn for more than twenty-four hours. True to her word, she was back in Kyle's room within her allotted thirty minutes.

At one point, she heard Peter's voice and her heart raced with hope. Surely he'd pop in to see Kyle as a friend, if not in his professional capacity. Yet his voice came and went past their door until at long last she admitted the truth to herself. He wasn't coming.

Bitterness rose up like a cancerous growth. She hadn't taken his sins out on Samantha—he shouldn't attribute hers to Kyle.

'Isn't Peter coming to see me?' Kyle asked. 'I thought I heard him outside.'

She struggled for normalcy. 'He's busy with his patients right now. You probably won't see him for some time.' Deep down she knew he wouldn't come, and she tried to prepare Kyle for the eventuality.

Dr Downey came and went twice—once in the morning and again right after the evening meal. 'As a precaution, I'm keeping Kyle one more night,' the kindly old physician told them. 'His latest PTT is nearly normal, thanks to the infusions Dr Caldwell ordered. The CT scan taken this morning looks good, too, but I want to keep an eye on his head. If all goes well, and I expect it to, you can take him home tomorrow.'

'Thank you,' she said.

For the next few hours Libby dozed in her chair while Kyle watched reruns of *I Love Lucy*. Suddenly her senses jolted her awake, as if an electrical charge had passed through her.

Peter greeted Kyle with a huge smile as he strode to the opposite side of his bed. 'How's my neighbor?'

Wearing an expression of pure delight, Kyle wiggled to sit up. 'You came!'

'Did you think I wouldn't?' Peter asked, wearing an exaggerated look of insult.

Kyle shrugged. Libby gritted her teeth to refrain from comment.

'I've had a lot of really sick people to see today. Since you were doing so well I didn't think you'd mind.'

'That's OK. I understand,' Kyle said.

Libby didn't feel as magnanimous.

'I hear you're going home tomorrow,' Peter commented.

Kyle nodded. 'Dr Downey said so.' He craned his neck to stare into Peter's face. 'Don't you want to be my doctor any more?'

After the briefest pause Peter said, 'I filled in for Dr Downey while he was out of town. Now that he's back he'll take care of you.'

'I'd rather have you,' Kyle said loyally.

Peter ruffled Kyle's hair. 'It isn't my choice, son. It's your mother's.'

Both of them turned to stare at her—one's expression

was hopeful, the other's cool and searching. The word 'son' was like a knife through her heart, but she didn't waver under their gaze. 'We've gone to Dr Downey for a long time. It would be best if we stayed with him.'

'But, Mom—'

'We'll talk about it later,' she said in her firmest tone of voice.

Kyle slumped in bed, his mouth twisted into a pout.

'Don't worry. I'll still see you from time to time,' Peter said in an obvious attempt to cheer him.

Will you? she wanted to ask, but didn't. Then she chided herself for her unkind thought. Of course he would. *She* was the one he couldn't bear to be around.

'Before I forget. . .' Peter reached into his inside coat pocket and withdrew an envelope '. . .Sam sent you something.'

Kyle accepted it eagerly. He ripped it open, then unfolded a piece of white paper. 'Look, Mom. She made a get-well card.'

Samantha had drawn a house, with a man and a girl on the front step and a woman and boy standing near the sidewalk. 'COME HOME SOON,' was written at the bottom of the page in large block letters. 'What a nice picture. You'll have to post it on your bulletin board with all the others.'

Peter bent down to hug Kyle. 'It's late. You should be asleep.'

Libby closed her eyes to the sight and pressed her lips together. She shouldn't be jealous of her own son, but she was. *She* wanted to have his arms around her; *she* wanted to lean on his strong shoulders and draw upon his strength; *she* wanted to feel his body against hers.

Her wishes weren't meant to be.

She opened her eyes as Peter said his farewells. 'I'll

see you soon, Kyle. Be good for your mom.' Without meeting Libby's gaze, he strode away.

Rejection had never hurt so badly. Instantly Libby knew everything between them had ended. For the first time in her life she understood how devastated and disillusioned Elaine had felt.

And yet Libby was lucky. She didn't have an engagement ring to return, announcements to make or explanations to give friends and coworkers. Blessings in disguise, perhaps, but blessings nevertheless.

A week dragged by. Libby had lost all interest in the holiday. Once a die-hard fan of Christmas carols, now she couldn't stand to hear them. In the end she refused to turn on the radio, except to catch the news, although she tried her best to hide her melancholy mood from Kyle.

'Can we go to the Elf's Workshop?' he asked one evening. 'Christmas is only ten days away. If we don't go now we'll have to wait until next year.'

She smiled at him. He'd been so patient that she didn't have the heart to postpone their excursion. 'OK. We'll go. But we have to be home early.'

He jumped up and down. 'All right! Can we go now?'

'Dress warm.'

'Can I bring my ice skates?'

Thinking of the trauma a fall would create, she shook her head. 'Better not. Maybe next time.'

On their way to the theme park a few miles south of town Kyle posed a question she hadn't expected.

'Why can't Sam and I play together any more?'

'Who said you can't?' Libby asked.

'Nobody, exactly. But whenever I ask to play with her, you say "not now". When Sam asks her dad, he says the same thing.'

'How do you know?'

'We talk at recess. Aren't you and Peter friends any more?'

'Of course we are. I imagine that Peter wants Sam to himself for a few days. You've been in the hospital and aren't ready for a lot of excitement yet. I enjoy the times when it's just the two of us, don't you?'

'Yeah, but I liked when all four of us did stuff.'

So did I, she thought.

In spite of the cold, many other Belleville residents and visitors filled the Elf's Workshop. Under Libby's watchful eye Kyle fed reindeer and an odd assortment of other animals, including a baby camel, several sheep and goats, rode the Christmas Express train through the park and visited Santa Claus.

He sang along with the carols blaring over the loudspeaker and exclaimed over the multitude of holiday decorations scattered across the grounds. Although outwardly she pretended to be excited over the festive atmosphere, her emotions had frozen harder than an ice cube.

'I don't know about you, but I'm cold,' she said, spying the bonfire near the shallow lake where a number of couples and children skated.

'Me too,' he said, pulling his stocking cap over his ears. Then he pointed. 'I see Peter!' He ran ahead, leaving her no choice but to follow.

Peter stood close to the burning logs, his collar turned up against the cold. His mouth widened into a face-splitting grin as Kyle rushed to his side. 'Well, look who's here!' he said heartily. 'Where's your mom?'

'She's right behind me.'

Peter glanced up and Libby swore his smile dimmed. 'Peter,' she acknowledged. 'Where's Sam?'

He motioned with his head. 'She's riding the train

for the hundredth time. I decided to keep warm while she's having fun.'

Libby made a snap decision. 'I'm going to get something to drink. Would you mind if Kyle stayed here with you?'

Peter winked at him. 'Not at all. Take your time.'

'Thanks.' Libby escaped. She hated to leave her son in his company but, knowing how much Kyle had missed him, a few minutes wouldn't matter. When she returned she hoped to have enough courage to finish her story. Maybe he'd accede to her wishes.

Peter sat on the nearby log and patted the spot next to him. 'It's been a long time. How have you been?'

His face solemn, Kyle stared up at the man he adored. 'Am I dying?'

For the first time in as long as he could remember, Peter was speechless. 'You are *not* dying,' he said forcefully. 'Where did you get that idea?'

Kyle shrugged. 'Mom says I shouldn't have excitement and she won't let me do *anything* except work on my model cars and play board games. She thinks I don't know but she cries a lot, especially at night. You and Sam don't come over any more either.'

Peter wrapped one arm around Kyle's thin shoulders. While wrestling with his conscience over the past few days, he'd maintained both a physical and an emotional distance in the hopes he could arrive at a decision objectively.

Unfortunately, his plan had failed. His soul-searching had made him realize that he still loved Libby, although his course of action remained shrouded in fog.

Kyle's question, however, was like the sun breaking through rain-clouds. The signpost in the road suddenly became clear.

'You're awfully sharp to notice the things you mentioned. I've been faced with some tough choices and I needed time to think, which is why Sam and I haven't visited.

'As for your mom not letting you do anything rough, it's because she's worried about you. Once she learns that you can scrape your knee and won't need to go to the hospital she'll relax. Just give her time.'

'Is that why she cries a lot too?'

Peter stared into the crackling flames, the red-orange and yellow tongues of flame dancing before him. 'Probably.' His instincts said it was more than that—*he* had caused her unhappiness.

'Then I'm going to be OK?'

'You're not dying,' Peter reaffirmed. 'After all we've been through, would I lie to you?'

'I guess not.'

Peter saw a familiar figure approach. 'Why don't you ride the train with Sam once more before we leave? I'll keep your mom company while we're waiting.'

'Great!' Kyle darted past a couple, then disappeared inside the little train station.

Peter motioned to the log. 'Have a seat.'

Libby sat, leaving a careful distance between them. 'Where did Kyle go?' she asked, placing the extra cup of cider on the log.

'For one last ride.' The glow of the firelight emphasized the hollows of her face and he knew she'd lost weight. 'I've thought a lot these past few days,' he began.

'And?'

'No matter what action I do or don't take someone will suffer.'

Her hand shook as she raised the disposable cup to her lips.

'I love you, Libby, and I was ready to follow your wishes. At least until a few minutes ago.'

Her spirits rose and sank in a matter of seconds. 'What changed your mind?'

'Kyle asked me if he was dying.'

Her rehearsed opening flew out of her mind. The cup in her hand fell to the ground, spraying cider over her tennis shoes. 'He what?'

Peter nodded. 'He says you won't let him do anything and you're always crying.'

'Oh, my.' Her chin wobbled as she stared up at the stars.

'He needs to know he can do everything he did before. What better way to be reassured than to talk to someone who's experienced the same thing?'

'Bryce doesn't have to be involved. There are hundreds of support groups. I'll find one,' she snapped.

'In Belleville? I think not. In the meantime, you'll smother Kyle in cotton. He's an active boy, for heaven's sake.'

'I'm aware of that. We're talking about *my* son. I know what he needs, what's best for him. *I'll* decide,' she said, pointing to her chest. 'No one else.' Her chest rose and fell with each breath.

'You're overreacting.'

'Am I?'

'Bryce can help Kyle.'

'Then he can do so without knowing Kyle's personal history.'

Peter shook his head. 'Bryce will figure it out once he sees the boy. They share too many physical traits for him or anyone else not to notice.'

'You didn't.'

'I was trying to survive another Christmas. I wasn't looking.' He paused. 'Although I have a loyalty to

Bryce and I understand your worries, the bottom line is what is best for Kyle.'

'Is it best for a child to learn that his father didn't want him before he was born? That now he does?'

'Bryce has a life of his own. Chances are that he'll stay out of yours.'

Libby met his gaze. 'And what if he doesn't? Who's side will you take? Will you support your cousin in fighting for custody?'

He hesitated. 'It may not come to that.'

'Any guarantees?'

'No, but if we're going to have a life together we can't have any secrets.'

She blinked, then laughed. 'A life together? You've got to be kidding. Do you honestly think we can salvage a relationship if you're instrumental in tearing my child away from me? After you've admitted you hold more loyalty to your cousin than to the woman you supposedly love?' She shook her head. 'If loving someone means inflicting pain then I don't want any part of it.'

'You don't mean that.'

'If the situation were reversed, how would you feel?'

'You won't lose Kyle. I promise.'

'Oh, Peter,' she said, her shoulders slumped and her voice weary. 'You're not in a position to promise anything. You'll talk to Bryce and after you've thought about the advantages Kyle will have you'll justify Bryce's actions.'

The pain on her face hit him in the gut.

'The best thing you can do for everyone concerned is to forget you ever knew us.'

The next morning Peter strode through the staff's private entrance, ready for a cup of coffee before he saw his first clinic patient. As he hung his coat on the rack in his office the receptionist walked in, waving a message.

'Dr Caldwell? Could you take care of something for me?'

'If I can.'

'Libby Brown called a few minutes ago. When she came in the other day Ruth was supposed to call in a prescription for her. As it turns out, Ruth didn't.'

After a sleepless night, thinking about Libby, to hear her name was like pouring alcohol on an open sore. 'She's not my patient,' he said evenly.

'I know, but—'

'Give it to Ruth when she comes in.'

'Ruth is off until after Christmas. Libby can't wait until then.'

'What about—?'

'Dr Downey is tied up in surgery. Today is the day Dr Moore makes rounds at the area nursing homes.' She waved the paper. 'You're the only one left.'

'A dubious honor.' He took the note and the folder she thrust toward him. 'I'll take care of it.'

He deposited his briefcase and Libby's file on his desk, hung his overcoat on the coat tree, then sat down to stare at the name on the label. Elizabeth Brown.

It was funny how he felt as if he were delving into personal secrets by reading her medical record. With great effort he tried to think of her objectively, just as he would any other patient. The only problem was that she wasn't any other patient. She was still the woman he loved.

He drew a bracing breath, then opened the cover. Everything was in order—the PA's clinical findings were neatly documented, along with the decision to continue the birth control pills for menstrual irregularities.

Intrigued by the diagnosis, he flipped through the

pages until he found the sheet he wanted—the initial visit health questionnaire. Few boxes were checked 'yes' and those that had been marked reflected childhood diseases and complaints common to women— monthly cramps, headaches.

One question, however, caught his attention. In the space for 'Ever Been Pregnant?' she'd written 'No'.

He turned to several other forms in the slim folder. All information correlated—she hadn't had a child, much less a son.

Peter jumped to his feet, rushed to the file room and returned with Kyle's medical record. The information transferred from his original physician, which covered his birth to age two, indicated his mother as Elizabeth Brown.

He rested against the back of his chair and stared straight ahead, unseeing. Why would Libby not admit to being pregnant when the evidence was obvious? Unless. . .

He returned to the reception desk. 'Call Ms Brown and ask her stop by and pick up the prescription. There's a problem and I can't call the pharmacy until it's resolved. As soon as she arrives let me know.'

If the receptionist thought his request odd she refrained from comment. 'Will do.'

An hour later he received a message that Libby was waiting in his office. He scrawled his signature to a request for X-rays, before heading to meet her.

She sat stiffly in a straight-backed chair, both feet planted on the floor. At first glance her face was impassive, but Peter saw the worry in her eyes.

'What's the problem with my prescription?' she asked.

'None,' he said. 'I just wanted to talk to you.'

'We've said it all before, haven't we?'

He shook his head and sat down. Resting his elbows on his desk, he leaned toward her. 'I want to know how the E. Brown who was pregnant in college is now Elizabeth Brown who's never had a baby in her entire life.'

Libby wilted before his eyes. 'Elaine, my sister, is Kyle's mother. After she died I took her place.'

Relief surged into his chest. He'd wanted to ask if she'd loved Bryce but, fearing her answer, he'd held back. 'Then you adopted him?'

She winced, fingering her purse handle. 'Bryce had told Elaine to stay out of his life. After the semester ended she ran into a friend of his by accident. She was terrified that Bryce would learn of our deception with the doctor and demand her baby. Consequently, we moved to Illinois and she checked into the hospital under my name.'

'So you're listed as his mother on the birth certificate.'

Libby nodded. 'We shared an apartment the entire time, but I didn't learn what she'd done until Kyle entered kindergarten.' Unshed tears glimmered in her eyes. 'Elaine must have had a good reason to resort to such drastic measures. I couldn't fail her, which is why I never told anyone. I quit thinking of Kyle as my nephew a long time ago. Even if I had five more children Kyle is and always will be my son.'

'Were you ever going to tell me?'

She nodded, her face a picture of misery. 'I wanted to right after his accident, but I never got the chance.'

Libby's confession touched his heart, but it was time old fears were laid to rest. He handed her the prescription.

'You want what's best for Kyle, don't you?' he asked.

'I've *always* wanted what was best for him,' she said

fiercely. Rising, she slung her purse handle over her shoulder and clutched the strap in a white-knuckled grip. 'Unfortunately, we disagree as to what that is. Like before, there seems to be little I can do or say to influence you.' She rushed from the room before he could refute her argument.

If only he could make her understand that, although he differed on how to best handle this situation, he wasn't the enemy. He knew what she wanted him to do—turn a blind eye. Yet he couldn't. He had to look after Kyle's emotional as well as his physical well-being. If talking to Bryce would help Kyle cope with his disease then Peter was bound by his medical oath to bring about their reunion.

He reached for his address book. Turning to the Cs, he punched a number on the telephone pad.

His cousin answered. Peter didn't waste time on polite conversation. 'I hope you're sitting down.'

Bryce chuckled. 'I am.'

'Do you remember Elaine Brown?' The dead air waves indicated he had captured Bryce's undivided attention. 'She had her baby after all. Another woman went to the doctor in her place. She didn't have an abortion.'

'Are you sure?' Bryce sounded excited, like the Bryce Peter remembered.

'As positive as I can be without DNA testing. He has the same hair color, the same features. He even has von Willebrand's.'

'I have a son.' Wonderment filled Bryce's voice. 'How did you find him?'

'Purely by accident.' He related the tale, including the story of Elaine's demise.

'I'll be there in a couple of hours,' Bryce said.

'Wait a minute. Libby isn't wild about the idea. Give me some time.'

'Sorry, cuz. Do whatever you have to do, but I want to see my son. Today.'

For the first time since he'd discovered his relationship to Kyle Peter wondered if he had indeed opened Libby's dreaded Pandora's Box.

# CHAPTER TEN

'THEY did what?' Sylvia stared at Libby in horror.

'I lost my job,' Libby patiently repeated. 'Supposedly our patient census figures aren't high enough to justify the amount of staff so some of us were let go.'

'It's absolutely ridiculous! You'd think they'd take into consideration if a person was a single parent,' Sylvia declared.

'It was all done by seniority. Those with the lowest received notices in their pay envelopes today. I happened to be one of them. My last shift is on December thirty-first. A nice way to end the year, wouldn't you say?'

Privately she wondered what other surprises would be in store today. Trouble came in threes and she'd already suffered two major blows—Peter had learned about Elaine and she'd lost her job. Holing up in her house for the rest of the week seemed wise.

Sylvia's wrinkled face took on more furrows. 'What will you do?'

Libby raised the cup of cocoa to her mouth. 'I prefer acute care work, but St Nick's is the only hospital within an acceptable driving distance. That leaves the nursing homes and the home health agency. Unfortunately, the salaries those places offer aren't as good, but I can't afford to be too choosy right now. Who knows? I may sell my house and relocate.'

Sylvia reached across the table and clutched her hand. 'Oh, I hope not. I'd miss you and Kyle terribly.'

'We'd miss you, too. You're like Kyle's grandmother.'

'There's no one else to hold you in Belleville?'

'If you're referring to Peter, I'm afraid not.'

'Then he knows about Kyle?'

Libby sipped her cocoa and lowered the mug. 'He knows.'

'And?'

'There are a host of other issues between us now. He wants to tell Bryce, even though I'm opposed to the idea.' Libby rose to pace Sylvia's kitchen. 'Don't you see? I can't trust him. If he'll override my wishes over something like this, what will he do in the future?'

She answered her own question. 'He'd agree with his cousin before he'd side with me, that's what. One Caldwell is formidable, but two are impossible to defeat.'

Sylvia shook her head. 'What a darn shame. I'd hoped and prayed you'd find someone special.'

Libby swallowed the lump in her throat. 'Me too.' Sensing that an emotional outburst would be forthcoming if they continued on this depressing topic, she pasted a smile on her face. 'Enough about me. Thanks for keeping Kyle's bicycle in your garage. He's going to be so excited, especially since he wrecked his old one.'

'I can't wait to see the look on his face.'

'Speaking of seeing the look on a face, is everything set for the meeting between Ralph and his son?'

Sylvia glanced at the wall clock by her telephone. 'Oh, my gosh. Tim should arrive in fifteen minutes. We'd better get over there.'

'You're sure this will work?' Libby asked as they trudged across her yard to the Upton home.

Sylvia raised her hands to reveal crossed fingers. 'No, but I'm hoping.'

'What's the plan again?'

'Tim will arrive by two o'clock. I'll let him in while you're keeping Ralph company. After we get them together you and I will slip out the back door.'

'What if Ralph doesn't let him stay?'

'He will,' Sylvia said, her jaw set with determination. 'I'll see to it personally.' Her face shone with merriment. 'I moved everything out of reach so Ralph can't throw anything.'

'How did you manage that?'

'Easy.' Sylvia grinned. 'I dusted his house this morning.'

'Won't he think it odd if we show up for coffee?'

'Not at all. We always have a snack around two o'clock, which is why I told Tim to come at that time.'

Libby halted in her tracks, her smile growing. 'You are a sly woman, Sylvia Posy.'

She grinned. 'I know, but don't tell anyone.'

Sylvia unlocked the front door, using Ralph's spare key. Soon they were visiting in the kitchen over a cup of coffee and a plate of home-made Christmas goodies. Libby was beginning to feel as if her insides would float.

The doorbell rang. 'Good heavens,' Ralph growled. 'This place is like Grand Central Station.'

A look of instant panic appeared on Sylvia's face. It disappeared before she rose. 'It's probably someone trying to sell something. I'll be right back.'

'Tell 'em I don't want nothing,' Ralph said in a loud voice. He leaned closer to Libby. 'Darn kids always think retired folks are made of money. Let 'em get a job and earn it the hard way like I had to.'

'Ralph?' Sylvia called. 'You have a visitor.'

'Hell's bells, woman! Bring 'em in here,' he yelled.

Hearing the excitement in Sylvia's voice, Libby knew this was her cue. She rose. 'Now, now. You don't want company crammed into your tiny kitchen. You'll be more comfortable in the living room.'

'Anyone who's too uppity to sit in my kitchen doesn't belong here, girlie.'

'Maybe not, but Sylvia wants you in there so we're going.' Without waiting for his agreement, Libby unlocked the wheelchair's brakes and pushed him forward. As soon as he cleared the doorway he stiffened. 'Tim?'

A man in his mid-thirties turned to face them. He stood a full head above Sylvia's five-foot-four-inch height and wore a skier's parka. Although his hair was blond, his bushy eyebrows and facial features resembled Ralph's. He grinned.

'Hi, Dad. Merry Christmas.'

'I can't believe it!' Ralph was clearly dumbfounded.

'I'd heard you'd hurt yourself and I wanted to see how you were getting along.'

Suddenly Ralph's delight disappeared and he narrowed his eyes. 'Come to see how close I was to dying, didn't you?'

Sylvia gasped and she bristled like a porcupine defending its young. 'Now, Ralph. That was a most unkind thing to say. Apologize at once or. . .or I'll never speak to you again!'

Tim touched her arm. 'Never mind, Mrs Posy. It's all right. I shouldn't have come.' He turned to leave.

Ralph waved his hand. 'Stay,' he said gruffly. 'Or I'll never have a moment's peace.'

Tim halted. 'Are you sure?'

Ralph fingered his sling. 'Yeah.'

Tim sat on the edge of a beat-up recliner. 'The house hasn't changed a bit. You still have the chair Mom tried to sell at a garage sale while you were out of town.'

Ralph snorted. 'Good thing I came back early.'

A moment of strained silence passed. 'It's good to see you, Dad.'

Ralph's eyes glistened. 'I'm glad you came, son.'

Tears came to Libby's eyes. The healing process had begun with Ralph's term of endearment, and she was both thrilled and humbled to share in the moment.

She quietly slipped into the kitchen. From the doorway she gave Sylvia a tremulous smile and a thumbs-up sign, before hurrying home. She wasn't needed; Sylvia had everything under control.

At least one relationship had been restored this holiday season, she thought as she hung her coat in the closet. Two, counting the one between Ralph and Sylvia. If only her own situation had turned out as happily.

A brisk knock interrupted her musing. Expecting to see Sylvia, she wore a welcoming smile as she flung open the front door. 'Don't tell me—' At the sight of her visitors, she cut herself off.

Instead of her elderly neighbor, Peter stood on the porch. The man on his left resembled Peter too closely to be anyone except Bryce Caldwell. Unreasonable fear swept over her and adrenalin speeded her actions.

She tried to slam the door, but Peter stuck his foot in the way. 'Please, Libby,' he said through the four-inch space. 'We just want to talk.'

'Issue an ultimatum, you mean.' Having told Peter the circumstances surrounding Kyle's birth certificate, Bryce had more information to hold over her head.

'No. No ultimatums. No threats.'

'I don't believe you. Either of you. Go away.' She knew she was acting irrationally but she didn't care.

'That's not an option. We'll stay on your porch all night if we have to.'

She glanced at the clock on the wall. It read two

forty-five. Coming to a quick decision, she opened the door and stepped aside. 'Kyle will be home in thirty minutes. I want you both gone in fifteen.'

'Fair enough.' The two men sat on opposite ends of her sofa while she perched in a chair across from them. At least Bryce wore a pair of casual trousers and a long-sleeved plaid cotton shirt, instead of a business suit reeking of power and success.

She noticed Bryce scanning the room, his attention riveted to the cardboard fireplace and the tree decorated with childish artwork. Daring him to comment about her second-hand furnishings, she raised her chin then turned her ire onto Peter.

'You certainly didn't waste any time spreading the news,' she accused Peter.

'It's my fault,' Bryce answered, his voice husky. 'When Peter called me today I couldn't wait.' He hesitated. 'I'm sorry about Elaine. She was a special person.'

'But not special enough to marry,' Libby countered. 'Or special enough to want the child she gave you.'

Bryce had the grace to look away. 'I'm not proud of the mistakes I made. If I could undo them I would.'

*I'll bet!* she thought unkindly. 'You relinquished your responsibilities ten years ago. You can't assume them now. I won't let you.'

For a few seconds her words hung in the silence like a cloud of smoke. Finally Bryce said, 'I'd like to meet Kyle.'

'No.'

He continued as if she hadn't spoken. 'A simple meeting. We don't have to tell him who I am.'

'No.'

Peter added his argument. 'I'll introduce Bryce as my cousin, who has the same condition Kyle does.

Kyle needs to share his worries with a person who understands—someone who's experienced what he has.'

'No.'

Peter rubbed the back of his neck. 'Why are you so stubborn about this?'

'My stubbornness kept us going when we had nothing else—no family, no friends. If I agree to your terms today, then tomorrow Bryce will want something else. First he'll take him for a ride in his Corvette. Next thing I know, Kyle will spend his weekends and summers on the Caldwell ranch.' She turned to Bryce. 'We followed your conditions. Elaine didn't name you as father or ask for child support. You have no right to barge into our lives. Why won't you leave us in peace?' She finished on a desperate note.

Bryce leaned forward. 'For what it's worth, I haven't thought beyond this meeting. I haven't made any long-term plans or decisions. I only want to meet my... Kyle. Can't you find it in your heart to grant one small request?'

If he'd called Kyle his son she would have thrown him out. Now she had to credit him with some sensitivity. Her resolve wavered. 'You two should have been lawyers,' she said.

Bryce cast an uneasy glance at Peter. 'I am.'

'Oh, no.' Her temples pounded.

'Strictly corporate law. This situation is out of my realm of expertise.'

Someone's watch beeped, signaling the hour. Peter mumbled under his breath.

She rose. 'Time's up, gentlemen.'

Peter came to his feet. 'Libby, won't you—?'

Bryce interrupted. 'She's made her decision. Thank you for your time, Libby. If you change your mind—'

he handed her a business card '—please call me. The number written on the reverse side rings my private office telephone. Only I answer that line.'

She took the card, without saying a word of encouragement, and stuffed it in her trouser pocket.

'Do you have a photo of him?' Bryce asked. 'Not to keep, just to look at?'

Libby studied him carefully. Intent on reading something sinister in his question, she didn't find anything. Giving him this much was the least she could do. 'In my bedroom. I'll get it.'

She returned a minute later and handed Bryce an eight- by ten-inch portrait. 'This was taken at school this past fall.'

Bryce studied the image. Eventually he handed the frame back to Libby. 'Fine-looking boy. You should be proud.'

His sincerity and humility caught her off guard. Yet she couldn't succumb to his charm like Elaine had. Disastrous consequences would result. 'I am.'

Before the men could reach the door Kyle burst into the house through the garage entrance. 'Hey, Mom. Where did the neat bike come from? Hi, Peter.'

She glanced at Bryce and then Peter, before looking at Kyle. 'What bike?'

'The one on the front porch. It's a ten-speed mountain bike, too. I'll bet it's a dream to ride. Whose is it?'

The guilty expression on Bryce's face told its own story. So much for the Caldwell humility. Bryce was already bringing gifts—expensive ones—before he'd even met Kyle.

Libby stared at Peter. How could you? she signaled with her eyes.

He sidestepped her to stand in front of Kyle. 'I'd like you to meet my cousin, Bryce. Remember, I told you about him. He has von Willebrand's, too.'

'Oh, yeah, I remember. Nice to meet you, Mr Caldwell.'

Bryce smiled. 'Call me Bryce.'

'OK.' Kyle turned back to Libby and fired his questions. 'I heard you talking to someone the other day about hiding a bike. Are we keeping it for someone? Is it Logan's? If it is, I won't tell. I promise.'

'I brought the bike for you, Kyle,' Bryce said.

Kyle's eyes widened. 'You did? Honest?'

Libby clenched her fists so tight her nails made half-moon impressions on her palms. Seething inside, she struggled to maintain a stoic expression.

'Honest.' Bryce glanced at Libby. 'Unfortunately, I didn't get a chance to ask your mom if it would be OK. You see, Peter told me about your accident and I thought you might be afraid to ride again. The same thing happened to me once, and it was a long time until I got back on a bike.'

'Can I have it, Mom? *Please?*'

'I don't know. . .'

'At least look at it before you decide,' Kyle begged, tugging on her hand.

Glaring at Bryce and Peter for putting her in this untenable position, she allowed Kyle to drag her outside and down the porch steps. There, propped against the garage, was the shiniest, fanciest bicycle she'd ever seen. Bryce had obviously purchased it from a bicycle specialty shop rather than the sports section of a discount store.

'It's beautiful,' she admitted, touching the padded seat. Seeing the awe in her son's eyes, she knew she'd never, ever be able to afford something like this. She hated the feeling the knowledge gave her. 'But it's too big,' she said.

Kyle grabbed its handlebars. 'No, it isn't. It's just my size.'

'It's too expensive a gift to accept from a stranger,' she clarified, emphasizing 'stranger'.

'Peter's not a stranger, and if Bryce is Peter's cousin then he's not a stranger either,' Kyle explained in his childish logic.

'Your mother's right,' Bryce said. 'But before I return it why don't you take it for a test ride?'

His face glowed. 'Can I? Please, Mom?'

'Stay in the driveway.' She watched him position himself on the pedals almost reverently. After he rode the full length of the concrete, turned in the street and came back the intense joy on his face was a heart-wrenching sight. The bicycle she'd purchased wouldn't evoke this same degree of excitement. Comparing the two, her gift would be found wanting.

'If Mr Caldwell—Bryce—wants to give it to you, I suppose it's OK.'

Although Bryce's face remained impassive, she sensed relief in him and in Peter. Kyle's war whoop of delight spoke for itself.

'You'll have to be very careful with it,' she said. 'Always keep it locked.'

'I'll register it with the police department, too,' Kyle said. 'Can I ride it some more?'

'To the corner and back,' she said.

'Mind if I go along to watch?' Bryce asked her. 'I need to adjust the seat since I wasn't sure about the height.'

'I'll get my tools.' Kyle ran into the garage and returned, brandishing a box-end wrench and a pair of pliers.

Without comment, Libby turned away, missing the glance Bryce and Peter exchanged. She stomped into the house, strode toward the Christmas tree, knelt down, then rummaged underneath to unearth a handkerchief-sized box. Rising, she ripped off the bow and wrapping paper.

Large hands removed the package from her grip. 'Give it back,' she cried, her emotions painfully close to the surface.

'Not until I know what it is,' he said, holding it out of her reach. He finished the job she'd started and stared at the Polaroid snapshot enclosed.

His eyes held regret. 'I'm sorry. I didn't know.'

She grabbed the picture of the bicycle she'd purchased and began to rip it into tiny pieces. 'Of course you didn't,' she snapped, 'because you didn't ask. It's only a reconditioned model. I was lucky to find one, but it doesn't matter now.'

'I'm sorry,' he repeated.

The Christmas she'd planned was ruined. 'What's next? A pony? And when he's sixteen and gets his driver's license—' Her voice broke. 'A Mercedes?'

Tears streamed down her face, and no matter how hard she tried the river wouldn't subside.

Peter tried to wrap his arms around her, but she slapped at his hands. Once she started she couldn't stop. He stood, allowing her to pummel him. Finally, her strength ebbing, she sagged against him. He embraced her.

'Go away,' she sobbed, clutching the lapels of his jacket.

'I can't.'

'You knew I'd refuse to let Bryce see Kyle.'

'Yes.'

'So you planned to come when Kyle would be here.'

'Yes.'

She wiped her tears on his sweater. 'I'm not happy with you or with Bryce.'

He rested his chin on her head. 'I know.'

'*I* wanted to give Kyle something that would dazzle him. He'd have been thrilled with the bike I'd chosen. Bryce didn't have to buy one so ostentatious.'

'So he went a little overboard. Under the circumstances, it's understandable. And forgivable.'

'Yeah, right. He's shirked his responsibilities for the past ten years, and now that it's convenient he wants to buy his way into our good graces.'

'That's not true.'

'Is it? I'll never be able to afford anything close to the gift Bryce gave. Especially since I was laid off today.'

'I heard.'

She pulled away from him. 'Did you orchestrate that with your friend, Eldon, so I'd gratefully accept Bryce's bribe?'

Peter muttered an expletive. 'Absolutely not. If you recall, I told you some weeks ago that layoffs were imminent.'

He *had* warned her, but she refused to credit him with altruistic motives.

'Now that Bryce and Kyle have met, will you allow them to see each other?'

She fixed her gaze on his. 'Do I really have a choice? You've disregarded my wishes before. I'm sure you will again if it suits your purpose.'

He squared his jaw. 'I'll repeat what I told you yesterday. You won't lose Kyle.'

She folded her arms. 'I want to believe you, but I can't. I don't have that kind of trust.'

'Fine. But be forewarned. I intend to stick around until you *can* trust me.'

'It would be easier for everyone if you'd cut your losses and move on.'

'I can't. I won't. We can have a great life together. I'm tired of being alone and so is Sam. I'll do whatever it takes—invest years, if necessary, to prove to you that I say what I mean and I mean what I say. *You won't lose Kyle.*'

Hope glimmered. 'Has Bryce mentioned what his plans are?'

'No, but—'

'Then don't make promises,' she said wearily. 'You don't have control over Bryce's decision any more than I do.' An unwelcome thought formed. She narrowed her eyes. 'Or do you?'

A hard glint came to his eyes. 'What are you saying?'

'It's oddly convenient that two weeks ago you avoided me as if I had carried typhoid. Now you're talking about a life together, working through the past— sticking with me until I trust you.'

Peter's lips thinned into a line. 'Are you accusing me of being in cahoots with Bryce?'

'Isn't it obvious? We'll be one big happy family. Meanwhile, Bryce has immediate access to my son without any legal hassles or nasty publicity casting a slur on the Caldwell name.'

Peter didn't answer. His squared jaw and the muscle twitching in his cheek spoke of his bridled anger. Yet his voice was calm. 'You're wrong, Libby. You've considered Bryce as the scum of the earth for so long that you can't see him for what he is—a man who made an error in judgement and freely admits it. Then again, you've probably never made a mistake and tried to rectify it, have you?'

He continued in the same breath. 'Weeks ago you mentioned something interesting. After I thought about it I knew you were right. Christmas is a time of healing and hope. The thing is—a person has to be willing and open to the miracles it offers.'

His comments stung. Before she could answer Bryce and Kyle walked in. Both were rosy-cheeked, their hair windblown.

Bryce glanced at Peter, then at Libby. His smile wavered as if he sensed the tension in the room. 'We'd better go, Peter. Kyle has homework.'

Bryce held out his hand to Libby. 'Thanks for letting me visit with Kyle.'

With some reservations, Libby accepted his gesture. She couldn't speak. Her throat was clogged with emotion.

Amid a chorus of 'thanks for the bike' and goodbyes between the three males, the two men departed, leaving Libby with an excited nine-year-old boy and her thoughts.

'I think it went well, didn't you?' Bryce asked as he drove toward Peter's house.

'She didn't call the cops to have us thrown out.' Peter felt Bryce's gaze.

'Libby means a lot to you, doesn't she?'

'Yeah.'

'I thought so. Kyle and I were going to come in but we saw you two were, um, occupied. So we went for another spin. Needless to say, I was surprised to walk in later and find you two glaring at each other. If the looks you exchanged had been weapons we'd be headed to the emergency room right now.'

Peter ran his hand over his face. 'She thinks I want a reconciliation so you'll have a foothold to gain custody of Kyle.'

'I suppose it's a logical assumption.'

'Libby called your gift a bribe.'

'I'm not surprised,' Bryce said wryly. 'After I saw their house I realized I should have chosen something more conservative. I didn't think.'

Although Bryce had been best characterized during his youth as impulsive, he'd changed after his relationship with Elaine. Caution had become his trademark. Hearing him admit to acting on a whim was an unusual and surprising experience.

Peter remembered the devastation he'd seen at one point in Libby's eyes. 'What *do* you intend to do? About Kyle?'

Bryce fell silent. 'I'm not sure. When you called I envisioned having him as part of my family. But before I make any plans I have to consider all the consequences. I made a hasty decision the first time. I won't do it again.'

Bryce stopped the car, but kept the motor running.

'I promised Libby that she wouldn't lose Kyle,' Peter said, testing his cousin's reaction.

'Are you warning me?' Bryce asked.

Peter's gaze didn't waver. 'I'm stating a fact. I told you about your son because you can help Kyle in a way that I can't. I also knew how much you regretted that part of your past. But Libby gave up a promising future in medicine and I won't allow her to have made the sacrifice for nothing.'

'So you think I should walk away. Pretend he doesn't exist.'

'Not at all. But if you intend to fight for legal rights to Kyle I won't support you.'